D0535450

THE COURAGEOUS PRINCESS™

THE COURAGEOUS PRINCESS™

VOLUME 2

THE UNREMEMBERED LANDS

BY

ROD ESPINOSA

DARK HORSE BOOKS

president and publisher
MIKE RICHARDSON

editor
RANDY STRADLEY

assistant editor
FREDDYE LINS

collection designer
TINA ALESSI

THE COURAGEOUS PRINCESS VOLUME 2: The Unremembered Lands

Published by Dark Horse Books
A division of Dark Horse Comics, Inc.
10956 SE Main Street | Milwaukie, OR 97222

DarkHorse.com
International Licensing: 503-905-2377
To find a comics shop in your area, call the Comic Shop Locator Service toll-free at 1-888-266-4226.

Library of Congress Cataloging-in-Publication Data

Espinosa, Rod.
Courageous princess / by Rod Espinosa.
volumes cm
Summary: "The plucky Princess Mabelrose uses brains and bravery when she is kidnapped from her home by a greedy dragon. Rather than wait to be rescued, Mabelrose finds the courage to save herself"--Provided by publisher
Contents: v. 1: Beyond the Hundred Kingdoms -- v. 2 The Unremembered Lands -- v. 3 The Dragon Queen.
ISBN 978-1-61655-722-5 (volume 1) -- ISBN 978-1-61655-723-2 (volume 2) -- ISBN 978-1-61655-724-9 (volume 3)
1. Graphic novels. [1. Graphic novels. 2. Princesses--Fiction.] I. Title.

PZ7.7.E87Co 2015
741.5'973--dc23

2014037517

First edition: June 2015
ISBN 978-1-61655-723-2
1 3 5 7 9 10 8 6 4 2
Printed in China

For those who sheltered the child inside them and kept its little mischievous spirit nourished with good books . . . and for those seeking that child again.

FINALLY! THE CITY OF AGBAHAR!
WE WILL FINALLY GET THE HELP WE NEED FOR SURE, SIRE!
MY HEART BLEEDS TO HEAR OF MY NIECE MABELROSE'S KIDNAPPING! BY A DRAGON, NO LESS!

BUT I'M SORRY, COUSIN. WE ARE PREPARING FOR A POSSIBLE GIANT INVASION. I CAN'T SPARE ANY SOLDIERS.
YOU CAN COUNT ON ME TO FUND MY NIECE'S RESCUE.
MY APOLOGIES, KING JERYK... EVIL APPROACHES US FROM THE LAND OF THE GIANTS...
I CANNOT SPARE ANY MEN AT THIS TIME.
BEHOLD, SIRE! THE TEMPLE CITY OF BATHALA!
HOMELAND OF THE HUNDRED KINGDOMS' GREATEST DRAGON SLAYER.
...BUT WE NEED YOU, PHILIPPE...
WON'T YOU HELP ME RESCUE MY DAUGHTER? YOUR NIECE?
WE'VE GIVEN YOU ENOUGH FUNDS FOR YOUR EXPEDITION.
WE HAVE ENOUGH MONEY. I NEED WARRIORS.
BRIGITTA SAID YOU WOULD COME WITH US.
SHE MUST HAVE MISSPOKEN.
COME NOW, PHILIPPE!

WE NEED THE DRAGON SLAYER WHO SLEW THE GREAT HALLEFERNES!
SHALATHRUM-NOSTRIUM, THE BANE OF PRINCES, WILL BE A CHALLENGE LIKE NO OTHER, BUT TOGETHER, WE CAN TAKE HIM!
THAT... WAS A LONG TIME AGO, BROTHER-IN-LAW...
I AM KING NOW... I HAVE... RESPONSIBILITIES.
I'M SORRY.
MY DEAREST HELENA,
HOW GOES IT WITH YOU? IT HAS BEEN MANY, MANY MONTHS SINCE MY JOURNEY TO THE SEER. IT HAS BEEN A DIFFICULT ROAD FOR US.
MY SEARCH FOR WORTHY WARRIORS IS NOT GOING WELL.
DANGER IS COMING TO THE SOUTH LANDS OF THE HUNDRED KINGDOMS. ALL MY COUSIN HASAN COULD OFFER ME WAS HIS PLEDGE OF GOLD.

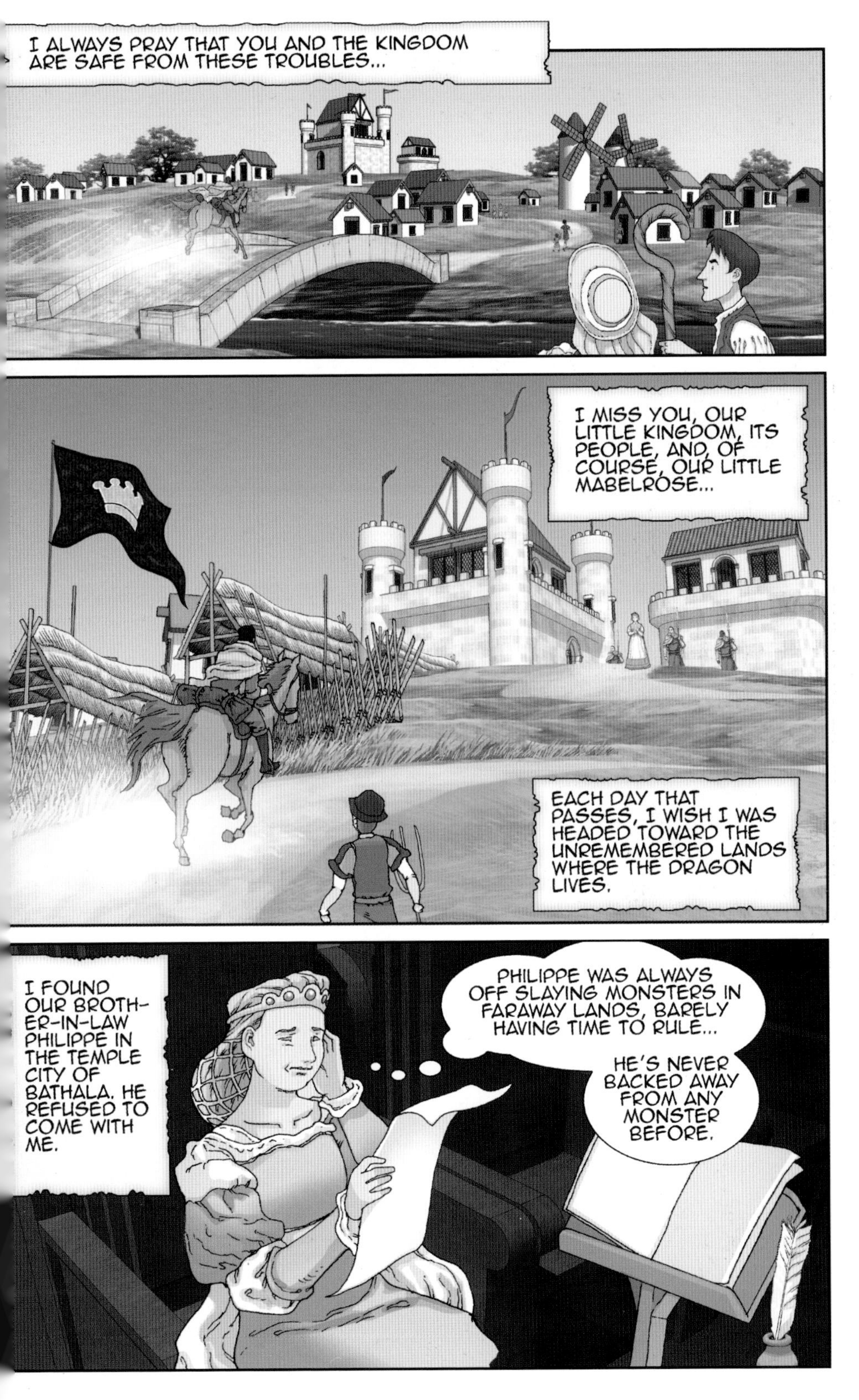
I ALWAYS PRAY THAT YOU AND THE KINGDOM ARE SAFE FROM THESE TROUBLES...
I MISS YOU, OUR LITTLE KINGDOM, ITS PEOPLE, AND, OF COURSE, OUR LITTLE MABELROSE...
EACH DAY THAT PASSES, I WISH I WAS HEADED TOWARD THE UNREMEMBERED LANDS WHERE THE DRAGON LIVES.
I FOUND OUR BROTHER-IN-LAW PHILIPPE IN THE TEMPLE CITY OF BATHALA. HE REFUSED TO COME WITH ME.
PHILIPPE WAS ALWAYS OFF SLAYING MONSTERS IN FARAWAY LANDS, BARELY HAVING TIME TO RULE...
HE'S NEVER BACKED AWAY FROM ANY MONSTER BEFORE.

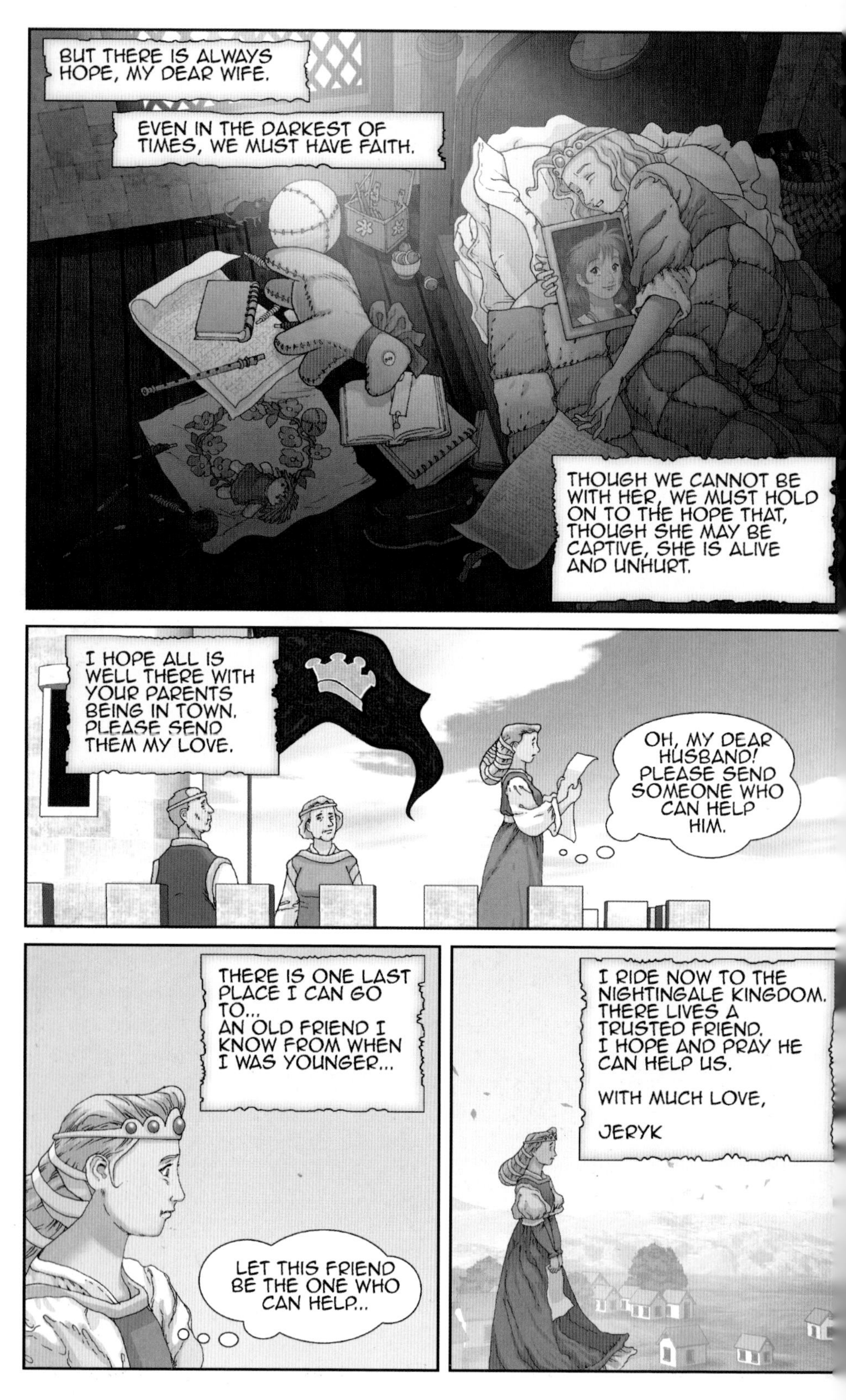

BUT THERE IS ALWAYS HOPE, MY DEAR WIFE.
EVEN IN THE DARKEST OF TIMES, WE MUST HAVE FAITH.
THOUGH WE CANNOT BE WITH HER, WE MUST HOLD ON TO THE HOPE THAT, THOUGH SHE MAY BE CAPTIVE, SHE IS ALIVE AND UNHURT.
I HOPE ALL IS WELL THERE WITH YOUR PARENTS BEING IN TOWN. PLEASE SEND THEM MY LOVE.
OH, MY DEAR HUSBAND! PLEASE SEND SOMEONE WHO CAN HELP HIM.
THERE IS ONE LAST PLACE I CAN GO TO... AN OLD FRIEND I KNOW FROM WHEN I WAS YOUNGER...
LET THIS FRIEND BE THE ONE WHO CAN HELP...
I RIDE NOW TO THE NIGHTINGALE KINGDOM. THERE LIVES A TRUSTED FRIEND. I HOPE AND PRAY HE CAN HELP US.
WITH MUCH LOVE,
JERYK

SHALATHRUMNOSTRIUM, YOU SAY?
YES.
NOSTRIUM... HMM... A MIDDLE-AGED GREEN... STEALTHY... LIKES KIDNAPPING PRINCESSES...
CONSIDERING THE YEARS THAT HAVE PASSED, HE'S PROBABLY BEYOND HIS THIRD MOLTING.
AT 800 YEARS OLD, "BANE OF PRINCES" IS PROBABLY MORE INVINCIBLE THAN EVER. WITH CLAWS THAT CAN CUT AN ARMORED KNIGHT IN HALF.
...FIRE BREATH THAT CAN MELT ENCHANTED SWORDS...
...COMMANDING UNTOLD HORDES OF MONSTERS...
AND HE HASN'T MADE ANY DEMANDS FOR RANSOM AFTER ALL THIS TIME?
I'M NOT WAITING FOR THAT BEFORE I RESCUE MY DAUGHTER.
INDEED, WELL--

YOU'LL NEED TWELVE BATTALIONS. MINIMUM.
500 HEAVILY ARMORED HORSES, FORTY SIEGE ENGINES, FIFTY LARGE BALLISTAS TO WARD OFF THE FLYING DRAGON, AND IRON CATAPULTS TO--
BOOTS, OLD FRIEND!
THAT'S TOO MUCH FOR ME.
I CAN'T DO A "STORM AND CONQUER" ON THE DRAGON'S LAIR! I NEED A SMALLER GROUP!
SMALLER GROUP MEANS A "SNEAK AND GRAB."
RIGHT.
YOU'RE GOING TO NEED SPECIALISTS AND EXPERTS.
FIRST OFF, YOU NEED A THINKER... NAY, A BRILLIANT STRATEGIST! SOMEONE WHO CAN OUTWIT OUR FOES IN ANY SITUATION!
THAT'LL BE ME.
...

"OFF WE GO, THEN... THESE NOISY HORSES WILL HAVE TO GO BEFORE WE ENTER THE UNREMEMBERED LANDS.
"I WILL TAKE YOU TO A MAN WHO HAS SIX RENOWNED SERVANTS...
"THEY MAY REFUSE... THEY ARE GETTING RATHER OLD...
"FIRST, YOU'LL NEED A SCOUT... SOMEONE WHO CAN SEE YOUR ENEMY BEFORE HE SEES YOU."
PAY IS NOT THAT HIGH, BUT YOU GET TO KEEP ANY TREASURE YOU FIND!
I'D BE HAPPY TO GO. NOBODY'S ASKED ME TO HELP IN A LONG TIME.
"SECOND, YOU'LL NEED A TRANSPORTER TO OVERCOME TERRAIN OBSTACLES."
AFTER WE DID THAT JOB FOR PRINCE VALIANT, WELL, WE ALL RETIRED IN COMFORT... BUT I AM BORED, SO I WILL GO WITH YOU.

THIRD, YOU'LL NEED A LISTENER.
ARE YOU MAKING THIS UP?
NO, I AM NOT. AM I NOT YOUR STRATEGIC THINKER?
YOU NEED SOMEONE WHO CAN HEAR THINGS YOU MAY NOT HEAR.
VISITORS... THEY'LL BE HERE IN TWO DAYS.
THE PROPHESIED HUNDRED-YEAR WINTER MAY BE UPON US... THERE ARE GIANTS COMING TO OUR LAND... THE COMMUNITY NEEDS ME TO STAY. I CANNOT GO, BUT MY SON HEARFAR CAN GO WITH YOU.
LOOK, WE CAN'T PROMISE HER HAND IN MARRIAGE. KING JERYK DOESN'T BELIEVE IN THAT OLD TRADITION. BUT YOU ARE FREE TO COURT HER--
AS SOON AS WE RESCUE HER?
--IN THE FUTURE.
THE FAR, FAR FUTURE...
I DON'T NEED ANY PROMISES OF REWARD.
I VOLUNTEERED TO HELP AND HELP I WILL.
THANK YOU.

WHAT'S NEXT, BOOTS?
WEATHERMAN. YOU NEED TO HAVE AT LEAST ONE WEATHERMAN. IT JUST SO HAPPENS...
YOU KNOW SOMEONE.
CORRECT!
LET ME GUESS...
...THREAT OF GIANT INVASION... TOWN SAFETY... YOUR SON WILL GO IN YOUR STEAD.
WHY, YES, HE WILL, ACTUALLY. AND MAY ALL THE GODS BLESS YOUR JOURNEY.
I H-HOPE WE'RE G-GOING SOMEWHERE WARM... BECAUSE IT'S REALLY C-COLD HERE...

CAN YOU BELIEVE THIS? EVEN CHILLY FOUND A WIFE!
WHAT'S NEXT, BOOTS?
A SMALL FORCE LIKE THIS NEEDS BRUISERS. EVEN THOUGH YOU NEED SECRECY AND SPEED, YOU NEED MUSCLE.
HOW MANY?
TWO, AT LEAST.
YOU'RE SENDING OUR SON?!

YOU'LL PUT OUR CHILD IN DANGER?!
WE ARE UNDER THREAT OF GIANT INVASION, SO THE TOWN COUNCIL WANTS ME TO STAY.
OF ALL THE IRRESPONSIBLE THAT IS THE WOR
DON'T START THAT. HE'S A BIG BOY
YOU ALWAYS DO THIS TO ME! YOU ALWAYS UPSE
NO-- NO! THAT'S NOT TRUE
OH, PLEASE
YOU AND YOU HAREBRAINE IDEAS ALWAYS
HE'S A WARRIOR! HE'LL BE FINE!
MMM... I BET YOU'D TASTE REALLY GOOD WITH BEAN CURD.
IT'LL BE YOUR LAST MEAL, I PROMISE YOU.
MA! I CAN DO IT DA! TELL MA I'M READY I CAN DO
LOOK, MAYBE YOUR WIFE IS RIGHT, CHIEF BIGEATER. THIS IS A DRAGON WE'RE TALKING ABOUT HERE. YOUR SON MAY BE TOO YOUNG FOR THIS.

WHAHAHAHAH! NONSENSE! JUST KEEP HIM FED AND HE CAN TAKE ON ANYTHING!
OOF!
HERE, SON-- CATCH!
KRAK
THAT'S GOOD.
THAT'S VERY GOOD...

WHOAAA! EATER, YOU ATE THE WHOLE THING?
SORRY, HEARFAR. STILL HUNGRY.
COULD HAVE USED SOME PARSLEY, BUT STILL... THAT WAS GOOD!
I WASN'T PEEKING.
YES, YOU WERE!
AT THIS RATE, I'LL BE OUT OF GOLD BY THE TIME WE GET TO THE UNREMEMBERED LANDS.
CHEER UP, OLD FRIEND! WE'RE MAKING GREAT PROGRESS.
THE ONLY PROGRESS WE'RE MAKING IS YOU AND THESE KIDS DRAINING MY COFFERS FAST.
ARE WE THERE, YET?

NOW THAT WE'RE HERE... I DON'T WANT TO BE HERE...
COLONEL PIB! YOU'VE COME A LONG WAY, OLD FRIEND! IT'S BEEN A WHILE.
GOOD TO SEE YOU TOO, GENERAL ODDSTARE.
THIS IS MY LOVELY WIFE! DON'T LOOK HER IN THE EYES, NOW! HAHAHA!
PLEASURE MEETING YOU BOTH, KIND SIRS.

SHE'S THE LOVE OF MY LIFE! WANT TO HEAR HOW WE MET?
WELL, WE--
OH, GOOD!
HOW WE MET WAS SO ROMANTIC...
I WAS CURSED TO TURN FOLKS TO STONE UPON MEETING THEIR GAZE.
SO I GOT BANISHED TO AN ISLAND.
"I TRIED TO ISOLATE MYSELF, YET MEN STILL CAME, INVADING MY HOME! THEY WOULD COME TO MY ISLAND WANTING TO CUT MY HEAD OFF!"
I NEVER MET ANY OF THEM IN MY LIFE. CAN YOU BELIEVE THAT? THEY ALL JUST KEPT COMING... WANTING TO SLAY ME, FOR SOME UNKNOWN REASON...
ONE DAY, A STRANGER WASHED ASHORE. HE WAS DIFFERENT FROM ALL THE OTHERS! HE WAS NOBLE AND KIND.

WITH HIM, I FELT LOVED AND PROTECTED.
"ONE DAY, A PRINCE FROM A FOREIGN LAND CAME AND WOULD HAVE SLAIN ME. BUT MY DEAREST LOVE DESTROYED THEIR WEAPONS AND SUNDERED THEIR BOAT! TOGETHER, WE DEFEATED THEM ALL."
...AND WE LIVED HAPPILY EVER AFTER.
VERY HAPPILY EVER AFTER!
AHIHIHEE! WE HAD THE BEST OF TIMES EVER AFTER!
MMMH! HAPPILY EVER AFTER!
AHIHIHEE! OH, BEHAVE YOURSELF!
NOT IN FRONT OF THE GUESTS, DEAR!
AHIHIHEE!
YOU CALLED, MUM?
AH, THERE YOU ARE, GAZE, DEAR! ALL PACKED UP AND READY?
YES, MUM.
BE NICE TO THE OTHERS AND STAY SAFE.
YES, MUM.
GODS BE WITH YE ALL!
ARE... ARE YOU OF AGE?
YES, SIR.

WHAT IS IT?
THEY ARE SO YOUNG... THEY SEEM TO BE MABELROSE'S AGE.
WE'RE HERE TO HELP THEM GROW STRONGER.
AS A FATHER, I FEEL LIKE THEY'RE STILL TOO YOUNG.
LOOK, HOW OLD WERE YOU WHEN YOU TOOK ON FORTY THIEVES WITH JUST ONE DONKEY AND A STICK?
YOU HAVE A POINT...
WHAT'S NEXT?
YOU CAN'T GO INTO THE UNREMEMBERED LANDS WITHOUT... A GUIDE.
GLORIOUS SIGHT!
SWEET MUSIC FILLS MY EARS!

...
OOH! WHAT IS MEM THINKING ABOUT?
NOTHING YE SHOULD BOTHER ABOUT, PUCK. GO AWAY.
METHINKS SHE BROODS BECAUSE SHE LOST HER MAJOR MAGIC.
OR BECAUSE SHE HAPPENS TO BE THE WORST FAIRY GODMOTHER EVER!
nyahahahahahahahah!

AWAY WITH ALL OF YE, BOTHERSOME TWITS! IF I HAD MY OLD POWERS, YE'D ALL BE GALLOPING GOATS!
BE SERENE, MEM. FAIRIES LOVE PLAYING JOKES, BUT THEY'RE HARMLESS.
WELL, MY SERENITY IS RUNNING LOW.
LOOK! LOOK! ROYAL VISITORS COMING!
VISITORS! PRINCES!
KNIGHTS! WARRIORS!
KING JERYK OF AGBAHAR HAS COME...

FAIRY-APRICOT FILLING!
YUM!
LADIES! MY NAME IS HEARFAR.
HEY, YOU TWO, WHY SO GLUM AND BLUE?
YOU THINK WE CAN MARRY FAIRIES?
GOOD QUESTION.
...

YOU'VE BROODED ABOUT THIS FOR MONTHS. YOUR SIGN HAS COME TO YOU.
I CAN'T GO WITH THEM.
YOU KNOW THE UNREMEMBERED LANDS BEST.
I WAS AFRAID YE'D SAY THAT.
YOU ARE PRINCESS MABELROSE'S FAIRY GODMOTHER. YOU MUST GO.
LOOK WHAT GOOD THAT DID HER. I'M NO FAIRY GODMOTHER.
YOU CANNOT HIDE FOREVER, MEM. YOU MUST FACE WHAT YOU HAVE BEEN AVOIDING ALL THESE YEARS.
YE ARE THE FAIRY GRANDMOTHER-- THE MOST POWERFUL OF ALL FAIRY GODMOTHERS! WHY DON'T YE GO?
I DON'T EVEN HAVE MY "ALL-SEEING EYE" ANYMORE... HOW COULD I EVEN TELL IF THERE IS IMPENDING DANGER?
CAN YE AT LEAST GIVE ME A STRONGER WAND OR SOMETHING?
I CANNOT GIVE YOU WHAT YOU LOST. YOU HAVE EVERYTHING YOU NEED WITHIN YOU...
EASY FOR YE TO SAY... YER NOT THE ONE WALKING INTO THE UNREMEMBERED LANDS.
I CANNOT RETURN TO THAT PLACE... I CANNOT FACE OROGIGANTUM AND... WELL... YE KNOW...

SAY, WANNA SEE THE FAIRIES WITH US?
NO.
...EVEN ODDSTARE FOUND A WIFE...
WHAT'S HE GOT THAT WE DON'T?
GAZE ISN'T INTERESTED IN FAIRIES.
IS GAZE A GIRL?
WHY WOULD HIS LORDSHIP HIRE A--YOU THINK SO?
THAT HAIR... GAZE'S MOTHER...
WHY DON'T W-WE ASK?
...I'M NOT LACKING IN MERITS, AM I?
YEAH, I HAVE PLENTY TO OFFER...
HEY, ARE Y-YOU A GIRL?
WHAT?
OH! YOU'RE A-A BOY, THEN?
ARE YOU MAKING FUN OF ME?
MAYBE WE CAN GO WITHOUT MEM.
WE CANNOT GO WITHOUT A GUIDE.
A-A GIRL! YOU'RE A GIRL, RIGHT?
YOU'RE REALLY INSULTING ME, AREN'T YOU?
HHSSSSS
HHSSSSS
I CAN'T BEAR THIS WAITING. CAN WE NOT RELY ON SEEALL AND HEARFAR TO GUIDE US?
THE UNREMEMBERED LANDS ARE NOT A PLACE TO GET LOST IN.
I-IS THAT ME THEY'RE CALLING?! I BETTER GO!
...

IS THAT HER?
YES...
OUR LITTLE MABELROSE. HOW I MISS HER!
SHE MUST BE SO FRIGHTENED, BEING ALL ALONE IN THAT EVIL DRAGON'S CASTLE.
THERE NOW, DEAR FRIEND... HAVE FAITH. WE'LL RESCUE HER.
LORD JERYK, SON OF ALAHDIN...

...
HEAL YOUR HEART, MEM. GO WITH MY BLESSING.
YOU WILL BE PROTECTED... ALWAYS.

UNREMEMBERED LANDS ARE JUST BEYOND THAT RANGE.
WE'RE CLOSE.
I COULD HAVE USED A FEW MORE DAYS AT FAIRY FOREST... FOOD WAS SO GOOD.

WHAT IS IT?
I HEAR THE CLINKING OF ARMS AND ARMOR... THE THUNDERING MARCH OF HEAVY, UNSHOD FEET...
"... GIANT, BY THE SOUNDS OF THEM."
THMMM

I SEE THEM...
OVER THERE!

DUST CLOUD RISING! IT'S A LARGE GROUP... A BATTALION, AT LEAST.

THEY'LL BE HERE SOON.

SEEALL, KEEP AN EYE ON THEM! TALLFEET, TAKE OUT THE OFFICERS.
AYE.
MEM--
COUNT ON ME TO SOW CONFUSION.
GAZE, EATER, BIG GULP, TAKE THE MIDDLE AND SPLIT THE COLUMN IN HALF. TAKE OUT THE HEAVIES.
YES, SIR.
POWER UP, BIG GULP!
AYE!
SHIVER, WATCH EVERYONE'S BACKS.
A-A-AYE, MILORD.
HEARFAR, COVER OUR BACKS. LISTEN TO THE BATTLE AND LET US KNOW HOW THE OTHERS ARE FARING.
AYE, COLONEL.
READY, OLD FRIEND?
I'M ALWAYS READY.

NOW!
CRASH
FEAR!
AIEEEEEEEE!
BATTALION LEADERS. THIRTY YARDS, SIX O'CLOCK!
GOT THEM!
thunk!
thunk!
TALLFEET JUST TOOK OUT TWO MORE OFFICERS. THE REAR GUARD IS LEADERLESS.
SO FAR, SO GOOD!

SHOWER OF CONFUSION-- GIVE EACH OTHER CONCUSSIONS!
SAVE US! HELP US!
SHORE UP THE RIGHT FLANK!
AYE, SIR!
EEW!
I'M A SNAKE! I'M ALLOWED TO DO THIS, ALL RIGHT?

HURR--
HEHE!
AAUGH!
ORGH!
BEEELCH! THAT COULD HAVE USED MORE ROCK SALT.

BOTH FLANKS ARE RETREATING! THE CENTER MASS IS IN DISARRAY.
"THE LAST GIANT HAS BEEN NEUTRALIZED! WE HAVE ACHIEVED TOTAL ROUT, SIR!"
STONE!

THEY'RE RUNNING FOR THE UNREMEMBERED LANDS. EVERYONE, REGROUP!
THANK YOU!
YAIEEE!
YAAAY! THANK YOU!
THANK YOU, KIND SIRS!
KIDNAPPING HAPLESS ELVES! WHO CAN BE SO DIABOLICAL?
SHOEMAKING ELVES. SOMEONE NEEDS A LOT OF SHOES MADE IN SHORT TIME.
BRICKLAYING PIGS... SOMEONE WANTS TO BUILD TOUGH STONE STRUCTURES...
WHAT FOR?

SHOEMAKING ELVES... BRICKLAYING PIGS... GOLDEN-GOOSE GIRLS... THIS ISN'T JUST AN ORDINARY RAID. WHOEVER WANTED THESE CAPTIVES SPECIFICALLY WANTS THEM FOR THEIR SPECIAL GIFTS.
THERE'RE FASTER WAYS TO GET GOLD THAN WAITING FOR EGGS.
IT'S NOT THE GOLD VALUE. I BET YOU WHOEVER CAPTURED THEM KNOWS THAT WHEN COOKED WITH A SPECIAL RECIPE, ONE GOLDEN EGG CAN MAKE ENOUGH SOUP TO FEED A THOUSAND MEN.
THESE MONSTERS WERE IN LEGIONNAIRE FORMATION. DRAGON ARMIES ARE STRONG BUT DISORGANIZED... NOT AS WELL EQUIPPED. THESE GIANT HELMETS WERE CAST IN A FOUNDRY.
THOSE BORORKS HAD UNIFORMS... STANDARDIZED PLATE ARMOR...
THIS IS SOMEONE WITH FAR MORE RESOURCES... SOMEONE WITH SUPERIOR ORGANIZATIONAL SKILLS.... SOMEONE MORE CUNNING... POSSIBLY MORE POWERFUL...
THIS ISN'T AN ORDINARY DRAGON ARMY...
TAKE THE FREED CAPTIVES TO THE FAIRY FOREST. IN OUR SADDLE-BAGS IS ENOUGH GOLD TO TAKE CARE OF THEM. TAKE THIS LAST MESSAGE TO THE QUEEN.
YES, MILORD.
OUR FOUR YOUNG PRINCES FOUGHT WELL.
THEY'RE BETTER AT THIS THAN WE WERE WHEN WE WERE THEIR AGE.
CAN YOU IMAGINE ME, A STREET THIEF, TAKING ON A FULLY ARMORED REGIMENT?
YET THEY ARE YOUNG. THEY WILL NEED AN EXPERIENCED LEADER TO GUIDE THEM.

AND A CAPABLE LEADER IS THE FINAL MEMBER WE NEED FOR OUR SMALL ARMY...
LUCKILY, WE ALREADY HAVE THE BEST. WELL DONE, OLD FRIEND.
THANK YOU, BOOTS.
COME ON, THEN...
"...LET'S RESCUE YOUR DAUGHTER."

Once upon a time, there was a land called the Hundred Kingdoms. It was a world filled with wonder, with touches of true magic here and there.
It was a land of enchantment... full of adventure and love.
One day there was a great celebration. Everyone from near and far was invited and everyone came.

For a grand party at the
Charming Kingdom
is not to be missed!
It was a joyous day, for three little princesses had been born and were to be presented to all.

The occasion was attended by many folks... including heroes from all over the land...

From the greatest and largest...
To the smallest and bravest... Everyone wanted to see the newborn princesses!

King Frederick and Queen Rosanda Charming were proud grandparents, for their three daughters were known for their courage, beauty, and skill.
Their three daughters were so renowned that princesses from other kingdoms admired them. And so on this joyous occasion, they all turned out in great numbers to see the newborns.

The fairy godmothers and their retinues all came out, for they too loved the Charming princesses.
First among the three daughters was...
Brigitta... the eldest and fairest in the land... Married to Philippe, known to be the greatest dragon slayer in the kingdoms. Mother to two new daughters... Giovanna and Anastasia...

Second was...
Helena... the middle daughter, simple and kind... Married to Jeryk, son of Alahdin... Mother to one...
...Mabelrose.
And then there was...
Ursula... the youngest... gifted and beautiful...
Married to none.

The little princesses grew up quickly. They would often play with each other while their parents went about their royal duties.
The twins, Anastasia and Giovanna, excelled at a lot of things. They ran faster than Mabelrose...

The twins were not only quicker but also taller than Mabelrose... And so they beat her and her friends at a lot of games.
Win or lose, Queen Helena always had a kind word of encouragement to say to her daughter... Served with a warm, delicious meal.
She knew Mabelrose was talented in her own way...

Mabelrose was indeed gifted... In unusual ways, that is!
She loved being outdoors and enjoyed learning about all kinds of creatures.
She wasn't one to complain about small hardships, either.

While the twins excelled in a lot of things that sometimes left Mabelrose behind, her mother was always there to cheer her up.
And so life went on for the young princesses...
Mabelrose did her best to keep up.
But as the three princesses grew up, they also grew apart...
It was not long before Mabelrose grew in other ways that soon separated her from other princesses in the kingdom.

Queen Helena was always there to teach her daughter things not covered by the royal tutors.
PEA KINGDOM
KINGDOM of FARRADIM
NIGHTINGALE KINGDOM
SHOE CITY
LAND of the GIANTS
DARK WOODS
And they always had time as a family to go out and have fun.
Mabelrose grew in her own way and in her own time... enjoying life as it came and savoring every moment.
The years passed happily...
And the young princess bloomed...

PRINCESS MABELROSE, MUST WE GO SO FAST?
HANG IN THERE, SPIKY! WE DON'T WANT THE OTHERS TO CATCH UP, DO WE?
REMIND ME TO STAY BEHIND NEXT TIME!

AHA! CAUGHT UP WITH YOU, FINALLY!
IT'S NOT OVER YET, KING ARGAILE!
BUT ON THE STRAIGHT, OPEN PLAIN, THE FLATRIDER'S FASTER THAN ANY OTHER CARPET!
AH!
ON CURVING MOUNTAIN TRAILS, YOUR ALDEMIA QUICKLEAPER BEATS MY MUSTAFARI FLATRIDER.
HA! MY LEAPER CAN ACCELERATE FASTER... AND I HAVE THE MOUNTAIN SLOPE ON MY SIDE!
GO, PRINCESS MABELROSE!
AYE, GRAVITY IS INDEED YOUR FRIEND--
--AS IT IS MINE! AWROO! HAHAH!
AWH--!
WELL, THIS OLD LEAPER HAS ONE MORE TRICK. HANG ON, SPIKY.
WAIT, WHERE ARE YOU GOING--?

AAAAH!
?!
OH! THANK YOU, MY FRIEND.

AAH! I'M STAYING HOME NEXT TIME! I'M STAYING HOME!
NO MORE CARPET RACES FOR YOU, THEN?
NOT ANOTHER PLUNGE LIKE THAT OR I MIGHT LOSE MY BREAKFAST!
I STILL DON'T UNDERSTAND THE POINT OF IT. WE'RE ALL GOING TO THE SAME PLACE. WHY DOES IT MATTER IF WE ARRIVE FIRST OR LAST?
IT DOESN'T. BUT IT IS FUN TO RACE AND BE FIRST.

WELL DONE! YOU HAVE GROWN IN SKILL AND FAIRNESS, YOUNG MABELROSE...
THE ALDEMIAS ARE THE LAST OF THE TRUE FLYING CARPETS. YOU HANDLE IT LIKE AN OLD MASTER.
THANK YOU, YOUR GRACE.
YOU KEPT UP WITH US VERY WELL, WALLY.
I'LL WIN THE NEXT RACE--JUST WAIT AND SEE.
WHEN SPRING ARRIVES AND THE ICE COMPLETELY THAWS, WE WILL MISS YOU WHEN YOU GO HOME.
I'LL BE BACK, YOUR GRACE. YOU ARE ALWAYS WELCOME IN NEW TINSLEY.

THERE'S THE WAY HOME... THE ICE SEEMS TO TAKE FOREVER TO MELT.
IN TIME. SPRING HAS COME. THE PASS WILL SOON BE CLEAR.
I WISH MY LITTLE LEAPER COULD FLY OVER THOSE MOUNTAINS. THEN, I'D BE HOME FAST.
ONLY CLOUD CHASERS CAN FLY THAT HIGH. NONE ARE LEFT.
BE PATIENT A WHILE LONGER. YOU'LL SOON BE HOME.
I CAN HARDLY WAIT...

...

?

!

?
!

...

THIS WAS... UNEXPECTED.
WORSE. IT'S NEVER SNOWED IN LEPTIA BEFORE. THE VALLEY HAS ALWAYS BEEN AN OASIS OF WARMTH.
I... I DON'T UNDERSTAND. ISN'T IT SUPPOSED TO BE SPRING?
WHAT DO WE DO?
WE SHALL CONSULT THE ORACLE.

PRINCESS MABELROSE! GOOD TO SEE YOU ONCE MORE, DEAR FRIEND!
I'M HAPPY TO SEE YOU AS WELL, TRICIA.
I'M LOOKING FORWARD TO HAVING A SLICE OF YOUR FAMOUS PIE.
ALL IN GOOD TIME. FOR NOW, GERDA AND I WILL TAKE YOU TO THE ORACLE.
IT WAS HE WHO SAW YOUR COMING AND MADE THE PROPHECY OF YOU FREEING US.
SO YOU HAVE COME...

LEPTIA IS FREE! FINALLY FREE FROM THE TYRANT!
YET... THE ONE WHO FREED LEPTIA IS NOT FREE FROM TROUBLE HERSELF!
HREHNNN... THESE ARE UNCERTAIN TIMES.
ISN'T LIFE ALWAYS UNCERTAIN?
HHNREAHHH... THIS WINTER IS NOT NATURAL.
YES, WE KNOW THAT.
WILL YOU STOP INTERRUPTING ME, YOUNG LADY?
SORRY! PLEASE GO ON.
HREHNNN... SHOW ME WHAT WE NEED TO SEE...

gulp... gulp... gulp...
DOOM! BEWARE, PRINCESS!
!
I SEE DARKNESS AHEAD! GIANTS! MONSTERS! EVIL!
YOU ARE IN PERIL!
gulp... gulp... gulp... gulp...
gulp...
DOOM! THE TIME OF THE EVERLASTING FROST IS UPON US!
FELL POWERS ARE IN THE AIR!
THE RULER OF THE LAND OF THE GIANTS IS COMING!
OROGIGANTUM IS COMING!
OROGIGANTUM?
OROGIGANTUM IS THE LORD OF DRAGONS!
THE LONG WINTERS HAVE ALWAYS COME BEFORE THE ARRIVAL OF THE GREAT BEASTS.
BE WARNED, PRINCESS... SHOULD YOU STEP OUTSIDE OF LEPTIA...
...YOU WILL FACE CERTAIN DANGER... AND PERHAPS YOUR VERY DOOM!

YOU STILL WANT TO GO.
YES. I HAVE TO TRY TO GET HOME. I MISS MY FAMILY. I MUST GO BEFORE MORE SNOW COMES.
I UNDERSTAND. COME, THEN--

"--WE MUST MAKE READY.
"WE WILL SUPPLY YOU WITH ALL THE FOOD YOU NEED AND MORE SO YOU WILL NOT WANT FOR ANYTHING.
"WE WILL ESCORT YOU PAST THE TROLL WILDLANDS.
Giant Vulture Mountains
The Land of the Hoomins, Elves & Fairies
Valley of Stones
Troll Wildlands
Dragon Peaks
Northern Leptia
"FROM THERE, WITH THE CARPET, YOU CAN FLY THROUGH THE VALLEY OF STONES. WATCH OUT FOR GIANT VULTURES. STAY INSIDE THE WOODS.
"IN PLACE OF THE RING OF FARLAN, I GIVE YOU THE LION KING'S PENDANT.
"IT WILL PROTECT YOU AND YOUR FRIENDS SO LONG AS YOU REMAIN CLOSE TOGETHER."
ARE YOU SURE YOU'LL BE FINE? WE CAN ESCORT YOU ALL THE WAY TO THE HUNDRED KINGDOMS.
MY THANKS, BUT YOUR PEOPLE NEED YOU HERE, YOUR GRACE...

"...AND YOUR SOLDIERS WILL BE NEEDED HERE. AN ARMY IS SLOW. I'LL BE FASTER ON MY LITTLE LEAPER. WITH IT, THOSE MOUNTAINS WILL TAKE A FORTNIGHT AT THE MOST."

FAREWELL, YOUR HIGHNESS. YOU HAVE BEEN A BLESSING.

ALLOW US TO GIVE YOU THIS SMALL HEARTH. IT HEATS WITHOUT FIRE AND WOOD AND WILL KEEP YOU WARM.
THANK YOU.

I AND MINE CAN COME WITH YOU.
THANK YOU, BUT WE WILL TRAVEL FASTER ON THE CARPET.
PRINCESS MABELROSE?
WELL, SPIKY, ARE YOU ALL SET?
...
?!
THIS IS NETTLE.
OH...
I AM THANKFUL I CAME WITH YOU FROM THE LONELY BRIAR KINGDOM. NOW I'VE FOUND A TRUE HOME HERE IN LEPTIA. I... I CANNOT LEAVE.
I SEE... I UNDERSTAND.
WILL YOU COME WITH ME TO THE MOUTH OF THE VALLEY?
YES, WE WILL.

HERE WE ARE...
FLY FAST AND HARD, BUT DON'T TAKE RISKS. STAY UNDER THE TREES TO AVOID BEING SEEN. DON'T TRAVEL DURING A BLIZZARD, AND FIND SHELTER FAST.
I WILL.
FAREWELL, SIR BOAR.
FAREWELL, MY LADY.
THERE... THAT COMPLETES YOUR NEW DRESS.
THANK YOU, TRICIA.
GODS SPEED YOU, DEAR.
GOODBYE, MABELROSE.
BE SAFE, WALLY.
KING RGAILE.
TILL WE MEET AGAIN.
WELL, PRINCESS MABELROSE.
MY DEAR SPIKY...
YOU'VE BEEN A WONDERFUL COMPANION.
YOU TOO... I--

OH, GO ON! YOU KNOW YOU WANT TO SEE THIS THROUGH.
!
KIND MADEMOISELLE, SPIKY TOLD ME ALL ABOUT YOU.
YOU WILL TAKE CARE OF HIM FOR ME?
I WILL.
NEVER FEAR! I'LL BE THE ONE TO TAKE CARE OF YOU, PRINCESS!
COME BACK TO ME SOON.
I WILL.

...
...
...
I CAN'T SLEEP.
I GUESS YOU MISS YOU OLD BED AT TH CASTLE.

I'M GLAD YOU'RE WITH ME.
GOOD NIGHT, SPIKY.
GOOD NIGHT, MABELROSE. MAY YOU DREAM HAPPY DREAMS OF HOME...

THOSE MUST BE THE GIANT VULTURES WE WERE WARNED ABOUT.
WE'LL USE THE CARPET WHEN WE'RE PAST THEM OR WHEN THESE WOODS OPEN UP A LITTLE.
KRAK!
WHAT WAS THAT?

AH, YOU SURPRISED ME!
WHO ARE YOU?
I AM RUMPLE STILTSKIN THE THIRD. LOST, ARE YOU?
NO. I HAVE A MAP.
GIVE ME YOUR BAG AND I'LL HELP YOU.
I CAN MANAGE BY MYSELF.
RIGHT THEN, IF YOU DON'T ANSWER MY RIDDLE, YOU MUST GIVE ME YOUR BAG.
WHAT? THEN, I CHOOSE NOT TO PARTICIPATE.
THEN YOU CANNOT PASS THIS WAY.
THAT'S FINE. I'LL GO AROUND.
NO, NO! YOU CAN'T PASS THAT WAY EITHER UNLESS YOU SOLVE MY RIDDLE!
FINE! WHAT IS YOUR RIDDLE, THEN?
WHAT HAS WHISKERS AND CLAWS AND HUNTS MICE?
WHAT... A CAT?
AGK! LUCKY GUESS!

FLIES AND HANGS UPSIDE DOWN--
A BAT?
ERP!
ER... THERE WAS A MAN AND HIS PET MOUSE... ERM... WHAT'S THE NAME OF HIS MOUSE?
THAT'S NOT EVEN A RIDDLE! YOU'RE NOT REALLY GOOD AT THIS, ARE YOU?
ARGH! NO MORE! HOW DARE YOU INSULT ME!
NO MORE PUZZLES AND RIDDLES. I'LL JUST TAKE WHAT I WANT BY FORCE!
OH NO, YOU WON'T!
SPIKY!
YEAAAOWW!
THAT'S IT! I HAVE HAD IT WITH YOU SNEAKY MAIDENS!
BRETHREN! COME FORTH!

UNCLE STILTSKIN!
YEAAA!
BROTHER STILTSKIN!
HO-HO!
?!
COUSIN STILTSKIN!
EYAAAA!
GRANDPA STILTSKIN!
WHEEEZE!
PA STILTSKIN!
GRAAH!
!
YOU THINK YOU CAN BULLY ME JUST BECAUSE THERE ARE SEVERAL OF YOU? I LEARNED A THING OR TWO UNDER THE TUTELAGE OF THE LION LORD OF LEPTIA!
GET HER!

whoop!
AAHG!
whap!
OUH!
twip!
ERK!
twip!
URK!
AIEEE!
OG!
HO-HO!
HA!
HRRN!
GIVE UP?

?!?
OW! THAT'S NOT FAIR...
HO-HO! GOT YOU!
HEY--!
SLEEP, YOU!
LET ME GO! THAT'S MINE!
IT'S OURS NOW! HWEEHEHEEEH!

YOU HEARD HER! GIVE THAT HERE!
OWHP!
?
SCRAM OR GET BEAT.
YOU! APPARENTLY--
"THIS FOREST ISN'T BIG ENOUGH FOR THE BOTH OF US," YES.
EAT BOOTS, FROG BOY!
EAT DIRT, STILTSKIN!

AIEEEE!

thump!

AND YOU TWO--
OWHP!
OUCH!

sock!
whak!
RUN AWA
BRETHRE
RUN AWA

ARE YOU ALL RIGHT?
HELLO! OH, AM I GLAD TO SEE YOU! YOU ARE THE FIRST PERSON--
"I HAVE SEEN IN A LONG WHILE," I KNOW! ME TOO!
YOU ARE A FAIR MAIDEN, AREN'T YOU? I AM PRINCE INGLE.
MY NAME IS MA--
NO NEED TO THANK ME! ONE GESTURE OF GRATITUDE IS ALL I ASK!
A KISS FROM YOU WILL FREE ME FROM MY CURSE!
CURSE?
I ONLY NEED ONE REWARD... ONE KISS FROM A MAIDEN IS ALL I ASK!
DO YOU MIND--
FREE ME AND I AM YOURS!
UM... I'M STILL--
KISS AWAY, FAIR MAIDEN!
WILL YOU STOP AND LISTEN TO ME?!

GET ME OUT OF THIS BIND!
YOU DON'T HAVE TO BE SO BOSSY!
NF!
WELL, YOU WEREN'T LISTENING TO ME!
OW! WATCH IT!
STOP WRIGGLING!
THERE, YOU'RE NOW FREE.
GRAH!
NOW, I WANT A KISS!
NO.
I NEED ONE SO MY CURSE WILL BE LIFTED!
YOU LOOK FINE TO ME.
YOU MUST--
NAY. I THANK YOU FOR SCATTERING THE STILTSKIN FAMILY, BUT YOU ARE NOT GETTING A KISS.
I RESCUED YOU!
IT WASN'T EVEN A GOOD RESCUE.
BESIDES...
...I BARELY KNOW YOU AND YOU'RE RUDE.
I AM NOT--!
GNAAH! S-SNAKE!
WHAT IS IT?

?
SPIKY! ARE YOU ALL RIGHT?
YES. I HEARD VOICES. WHO WERE YOU TALKING TO?
PRINCE INGLE. HE WAS JUST HERE...
PRINCE INGLE? WHERE ARE YOU?
!
I-I'M HERE.
IS THAT YOU, PRINCE INGLE?
I TOLD YOU I WAS CURSED.
THIS IS MY FRIEND SPIKY.
DO YOU WANT TO COME WITH US?
YES, I WOULD. I--
?!

THERE THEY ARE, BRETHREN! GET THEM!
AIEE! RUN! RUN!
TO THE CARPET!
FASTER! THEY'RE GAINING!
WE'LL GET AWAY FASTER ON THE OPEN GROUND.
WAIT--
GOOD RIDDANCE TO THOSE LICE!

?
PRINCESS--
MABELROSE--
THE FOREST--!
THE FROG TURNED INTO A BOY!
WE'LL BE SAFE IN THE FOREST!
YOU CHOSE A BAD TIME TO REJOIN US, PRINCE INGLE. NOW WE'RE HEAVIER!

TURN BACK INTO A FROG, INGLE!
I CAN'T CONTROL MY CURSE!
TURN INTO THOSE TREES BEFORE--
BEFORE--?
OH!
THE VULTURES! WE'RE DONE FOR!

RAAAWWWK
AAH! FASTER! FASTER!

HANG ON!
AIEEE!
WRAAK!
SQUAAAWWWWWK
AAAAAH!
plip

AAAH! ET IN THE WOODS!
AGH-- OFF!
AAH! ALMOST THERE! COME ON, LITTLE LEAPER! GO! GO--
KRAKK
--GO!
BWUFF
FOOMP
AIE!
OH!
OUCH!
WELL, PRINCE INGLE... WE'RE BACK IN THE WOODS...

MY MANY THANKS FOR HAVING ME ALONG, MABELROSE. I HAVEN'T BEEN THIS WARM IN A LONG TIME.
YOUR CARPET IS AMAZING... I DID NOT KNOW THEY CAN TURN INTO TENTS.
ONLY THE ALDEMIA QUICKLEAPERS CAN DO THAT, PRINCE INGLE.
SO WARM AND TOASTY IN HERE.
AND THAT BAG! I CAN'T BELIEVE ALL THESE THINGS CAN FIT IN THERE.
THE FORMER LEPTIAN KING PUT HIS ENTIRE HOARD OF GOLD INSIDE IT ONCE. EVEN AFTER I EMPTIED IT, SOMETIMES A GOLD COIN STILL POPS OUT EVERY NOW AND THEN.
THANKS FOR SHARING YOUR FOOD WITH ME.
YOU'RE WELCOME

WHERE ARE YOU FROM, PRINCE INGLE?
I CAME FROM THE HILLSHIRE KINGDOM.
I WAS SEPARATED FROM MY FATHER AND MOTHER DURING A SEA STORM.
I WAS SEPARATED FROM MY FAMILY, TOO.
HOW DID YOU END UP HERE?
I WAS CAPTURED AND CURSED BY A WARLOCK. I ESCAPED AND FOUND MYSELF HERE, UNABLE TO CLIMB THE TALL PEAKS THAT SURROUND THIS VALLEY.
THE ONLY WAY OUT OF THIS VALLEY IS THROUGH THE LAND OF THE GIANTS.
I WAS ALMOST GIANT DINNER, SO I DARE NOT TRY TO GO BACK THERE.
WHAT ABOUT YOU, MABELROSE? WHY ARE YOU HERE?
A DRAGON CALLED SHALATHRUMNOSTRIUM CAPTURED ME AND TOOK ME TO HIS CASTLE...
A-A DRAGON?!

...I THINK HE WAS FRIENDS WITH THE GIANTS. HE SAID THEY WERE BRINGING HIM GOLD. SO ONE DAY, WHEN HE FLEW OUT TO MEET THEM, I ESCAPED HIS CASTLE...
YOU ESCAPED A DRAGON'S CASTLE?!
...ANYWAY, SPIKY SAVED ME FROM THE RIVER. HE LED THE MUNKENS TO WHERE I WAS HIDDEN...
...THE MUNKENS SHELTERED ME AND TOOK CARE OF ME AS IF I WERE ONE OF THEIR OWN...
YOU ARE LUCKY TO HAVE SO MANY FRIENDS. IT'S BEEN AGES SINCE I TASTED BREAD...
...AFTER THAT, I LIVED WITH THE LEPTIANS FOR A WHILE. THERE, I MET KING ARGAILE, WHO GAVE ME MAPS TO THIS VALLEY...
YOU'VE BEEN THROUGH A LOT!
OH, SHE'S TOO MODEST. SHE LEFT OUT THE PARTS WHERE SHE FREED THE LEPTIANS FROM A TYRANT AND SLEW THE DRAGON NOSTRIUM USING A FLUTE.
?!

IT STILL AMAZES ME...
I SPENT A LONG TIME TRYING TO FIND A PATH THROUGH THESE MOUNTAINS...
THEY KEPT ME IN THAT VALLEY. NOW WE JUST FLY OVER THEM.
YOU'RE LUCKY I'M HERE TO BRING YOU OUT.
YOU'RE LUCKY I SAVED YOU JUST IN TIME FROM THOSE THIEVES.
SO, UM... ONCE WE LEAVE THE UNREMEMBERED LANDS... MAY I ESCORT YOU ALL THE WAY TO NEW TINSLEY?
I WOULD LIKE THAT VERY MUCH, PRINCE INGLE.
OH, LOOK!

WE'RE HERE, INGLE! WE'VE LEFT THE UNREMEMBERED LANDS!
UNLESS MY EYES TRICK ME, THAT THERE IS THE LAND OF THE HUNDRED KINGDOMS!
THE TREES... SO MANY FRAGRANT TREES.
IT'S BEEN SO LONG... I... I'VE DREAMED OF THIS MOMENT.
COME, THEN...
...LET US RIDE DOWN!
YES!

WE'RE HERE, SPIKY!
WE'RE FREE! WE'RE GOING HOME!
IS IT ME OR DOES EVEN THE WATER TASTE SWEETER? 
MY FIRST DRINK OF WATER WITHOUT WATCHING FOR MONSTERS...

WE DID IT, SPIKY! HAHAHA!
WE'RE HERE! WELCOME TO THE HUNDRED KINGDOMS!
SHALL WE GO TO YOUR HOME, THEN?
YES. MY FAMILY WILL GET SUCH A SURPRISE.
THAT'S THE GRANITE BRIDGE. THIS IS MY FIRST TIME SEEING IT. IT'S THE MAIN ROAD LINKING THE UNREMEMBERED LANDS TO THE HUNDRED KINGDOMS. IT WAS BUILT LONG AGO BY THE RULERS OF THE BRIAR KINGDOM FOR TRADE... NOW IT'S JUST A PATH FOR GOATS.
AND GIANTS. WE'D BEST FOLLOW ANOTHER WAY UNTIL WE GET TO THE FAIRY FOREST.
LOOK, A DEER TRAIL. FOLLOW ME.
ONCE YOU ARE SAFE, I WILL TRY TO FIND MY FAMILY.
WE'LL HELP YOU.
UH... PRINCESS MABELROSE?
OUH...
OH, WHAT IS THIS?

IT'S A CAMP...
SOMEONE'S BEEN HERE...
RECENTLY, FROM THE SMELL OF IT.
THEY LEFT IN A HURRY.
...
HUH?!
PRINCESS!
WHAT IS IT?
NO... IT... IT CAN'T BE...
IT IS! THAT'S THE PATCH I SEWED ON MYSELF! THIS IS MY FATHER'S!
IF IT'S HERE, THEN--

PRINCESS MABELROSE!
YE'RE HERE! YE'RE FREE! OH! GODS ARE GOOD!
MABELROSE!
FAIRY GODMOTHER MEM? HOW...? WHERE DID YOU COME FROM?
IT IS YE, MABELROSE! OH, I DON'T BELIEVE IT. IT IS YE!
AM I SO GLAD TO SEE YE! GODS ARE GOOD! LOOK AT YOU! FREE FROM THE DRAGON! BUT HOW?
AND OOH... YE'RE ALL GROWN PRETTY!
T-THANKS, MEM...
THESE ARE MY FRIENDS. THAT'S SPIKY, WHO'S BEEN WITH ME SINCE I ESCAPED THE DRAGON.
AND THAT'S PRINCE INGLE.

IT'S SUCH A RELIEF TO SEE YOU, MEM... THIS IS--?
OH, YES... THAT'S... THAT'S YOUR FATHER'S, AYE.
HE WAS HERE?
AYE... WE WERE GOING TO RESCUE YE. HE HAD A MIGHTY BAND OF HEROES WITH HIM... AND FOUR YOUNG PRINCES SWORN TO FREE YE.
DID YOU HEAR THAT, SPIKY? NOSTRIUM WAS WRONG. FOUR PRINCES CAME TO RESCUE ME.
THEY WERE COMING FOR ME. NOT ONE, NOT TWO... NOT THREE...
FOUR.
FOUR PRINCES...
...
WHAT HAPPENED TO THEM?
I...
I WAS TO GUIDE THEM TO THE UNREMEMBERED LANDS.
WE FAILED. WE WERE ATTACKED.
OH, NO... NO...
TELL US MORE...
THEY CAME AT DAWN...

ANY IDEAS, BOOTS?
FIGHT AND PERISH... NEGOTIATE... SURRENDER AND LIVE. NO GOOD OPTIONS.
OUR CHANCES?
WELL...
...HE WHO CAN HEAR EVERYTHING DIDN'T HEAR ANYTHING...
...HE WHO CAN SEE FARTHEST DIDN'T SEE THIS COMING...
...OBVIOUSLY, HE JUST SLEPT THROUGH IT...
...WE'VE BEEN OVERWHELMED WITH SUPERIOR MAGIC...
...NUMBERS...
...AND BRUTE STRENGTH.
OUR CHANCES ARE NOT GOOD.
I SHOULD HAVE KNOWN IT WAS YOU...

WELL MET, COLONEL PIB.
VERY FEW MEET ME AND LIVE TO TELL ABOUT IT.
ME BEING ONE OF THE VERY FEW, NATURALLY.
YOU NEED NOT TROUBLE YOURSELF, GREAT ONE.
YOU'LL BE GLAD TO KNOW WE'RE NOT HERE TO FIGHT YOU.
OH HO! TRULY?
TRULY. WE ARE HERE ON OTHER BUSINESS, NOT YOURS.
INDEED? DIDN'T YOU JUST AMBUSH MY TROOPS?
AND ISN'T IT MY BUSINESS WHEN I FIND YOU SNEAKING INTO MY REALM?
WELL, YOU WILL GET YOUR WISH. INTO THE UNREMEMBERED LANDS WITH YOU.
IS THIS ALL OF THEM? GOOD. BRING THEM TO THE CLOUD CASTLE.

SURRENDER? WE CAN'T JUST GIVE UP.
THEY'LL MOST LIKELY BRING US DEEPER INTO THE UNREMEMBERED LANDS... AT LEAST WE'LL BE, WELL, SOMEWHAT CLOSER TO MABELROSE...
WE MUST, IF WE WANT TO LIVE.
THEY WANT US ALIVE. ELSE THEY WOULD NOT HAVE BOTHERED TO SNEAK IN AND WAKE US UP.
"...AGAINST SUCH MIGHT, WE CANNOT HOPE TO PREVAIL."

IT'S TIME TO SURVIVE. BESIDES... WE ARE DEALING WITH A CLASS FIVE...
...A DRAGON THAT HAS PASSED ITS FIFTH MOLTING...
"YES, I KNOW THIS MONSTER WELL. HOW CAN I EVER FORGET SURVIVING AN ENCOUNTER WITH--"

OROGIGANTUM???
IS THERE ANYONE WHO CAN HELP US FIND FATHER?
NO, PRINCESS... WE... WE CAN'T...
WE MUST.
BUT YE'RE HERE! YE'RE ALREADY SAFE. GO HOME! YOUR FATHER ALREADY SACRIFICED HIMSELF FOR YOU.
I CAN'T.
I CAN'T JUST LEAVE HIM. HE'S MY FATHER. HE CAME TO RESCUE ME.
THERE MUST BE SOMEONE... UNCLE PHILIPPE? FATHER'S COUSINS?
NO... EVERYONE WHO CAN COME ALREADY CAME. YOUR FATHER SEARCHED THE ENTIRE KINGDOM... THERE'S NOBODY LEFT.
B-BUT... IT CAN'T END THIS WAY...
I CAN'T GO HOME WITHOUT FATHER...
AREN'T THE KINGDOMS FILLED WITH KNIGHTS? DRAGON SLAYERS?
NONE. ALL THE KINGDOMS ARE PREPARING AGAINST THE GIANTS.

WE WOULD HAVE MET HERE HAD I BEEN QUICKER... I HAD THE CARPET... I SHOULD HAVE ARRIVED SOONER... I COULD HAVE...
THERE WAS NOTHING YE COULD HAVE DONE, PRINCESS.
WE MUST GO... GO RESCUE THEM.
WHAT? NO, NO! YOU CANNOT DO THAT!
GO BACK?! INTO THE UNREMEMBERED LANDS???
ARE YOU WITH ME, PRINCE INGLE?
AGAINST GIANTS? NO!
I AM GOING HOME!
YOU'RE A GOOD FIGHTER. WE NEED YOU.
AGAINST THE LORD OF DRAGONS?! WHAT CHANCE DO WE HAVE IF YOUR FATHER AND HIS KNIGHTS FAILED?
I CANNOT ALLOW IT. I ALREADY FAILED YOU ONCE WHEN SHALATHRUM-NOSTRIUM GOT TO YOU...

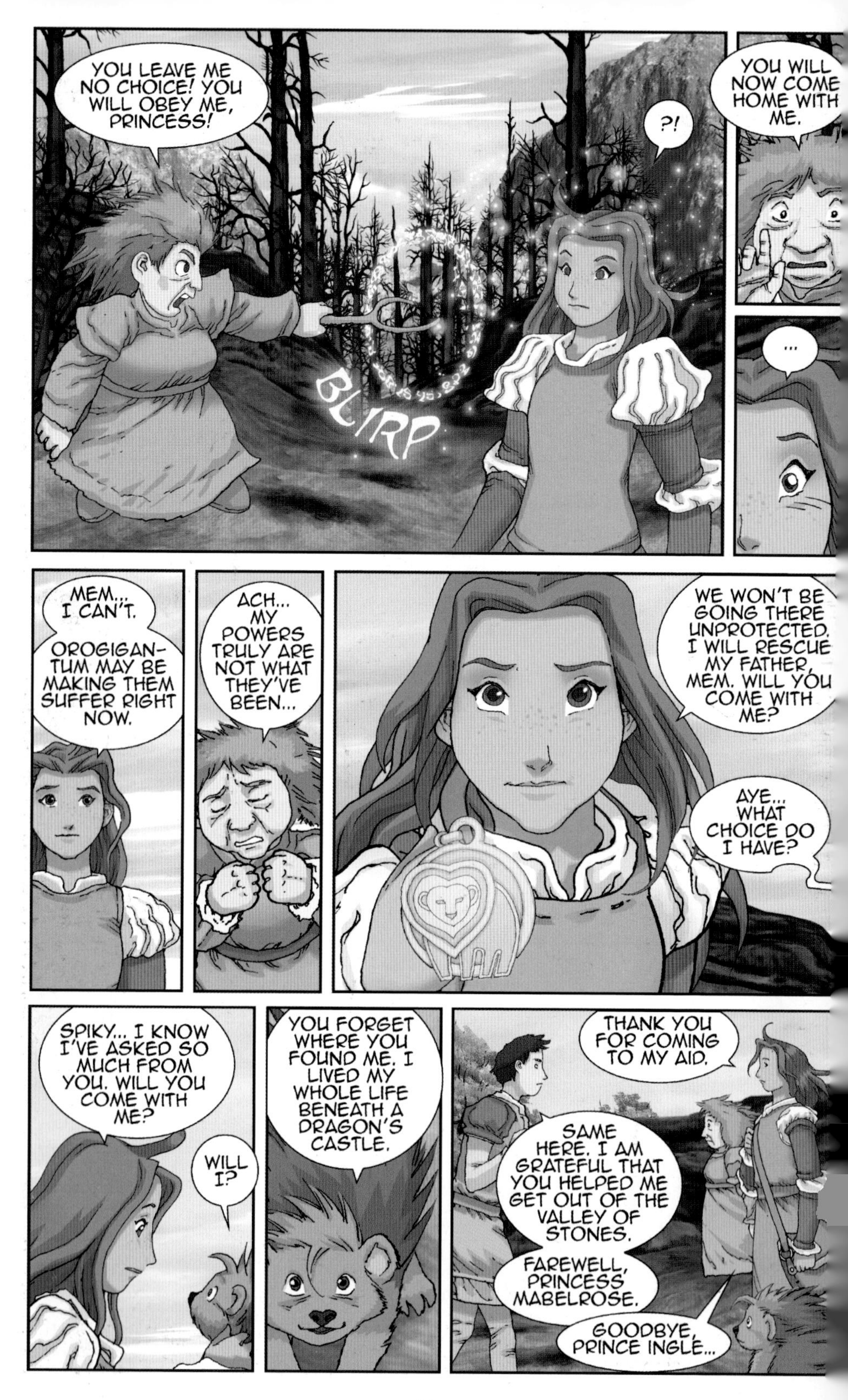
YOU LEAVE ME NO CHOICE! YOU WILL OBEY ME, PRINCESS!
BLIRP
?!
YOU WILL NOW COME HOME WITH ME.
...
MEM... I CAN'T.
OROGIGAN-TUM MAY BE MAKING THEM SUFFER RIGHT NOW.
ACH... MY POWERS TRULY ARE NOT WHAT THEY'VE BEEN...
WE WON'T BE GOING THERE UNPROTECTED. I WILL RESCUE MY FATHER, MEM. WILL YOU COME WITH ME?
AYE... WHAT CHOICE DO I HAVE?
SPIKY... I KNOW I'VE ASKED SO MUCH FROM YOU. WILL YOU COME WITH ME?
WILL I?
YOU FORGET WHERE YOU FOUND ME. I LIVED MY WHOLE LIFE BENEATH A DRAGON'S CASTLE.
THANK YOU FOR COMING TO MY AID.
SAME HERE. I AM GRATEFUL THAT YOU HELPED ME GET OUT OF THE VALLEY OF STONES.
FAREWELL, PRINCESS MABELROSE.
GOODBYE, PRINCE INGLE...

WE CAN'T JUST SPLIT UP. CAN'T WE STAY TOGETHER? COME, PRINCE INGLÉ, WE--
HOME AND SAFETY LIE THIS WAY!
GO BACK THERE, IF YOU LIKE... AND BE GIANT STEW!
LEAVE US, THEN. WE DON'T NEED YOU.

WE MUST BE QUIET AND QUICK NOW... I HAVE BEEN TASKED TO GUIDE YOUR FATHER TO NOSTRIUM'S CASTLE... BUT OROGIGANTUM LIVES IN THE SOUTH... IN THE CLOUD KINGDOM.
BEYOND THE LAND OF THE GIANTS...
WE'LL STAY OFF THE MAIN ROAD... FLY AS LITTLE AS POSSIBLE. OROGIGANTUM HAS EYES EVERYWHERE.
LISTEN NOW, MY DEAR. THERE'RE MANY KINDS OF GIANTS HERE...
...THERE'RE BIG GIANTS... THEN THERE'RE EVEN BIGGER GIANTS.... THERE'RE GIANTS THAT CAN SEE FAR AND IN DARKNESS... THERE'RE ALSO GIANTS THAT CAN SMELL YE A LONG WAY OFF.

HOW DO YOU KNOW SO MUCH ABOUT THE LAND OF THE GIANTS?
I USED TO... ERM, LIVE HERE.
THE WINTER BLOOMS CAN COVER OUR SCENT FROM THE SNIFFERS. GATHER AS MUCH AS YOU CAN.
IT'S NOT TOO LATE TO TURN BACK, MABELROSE... NOSTRIUM HAD A DOZEN GIANTS. YE PROBABLY SAW THEM. OROGIGANTUM COMMANDS THOUSANDS.
WE'LL STAY HIDDEN. FATHER'S GROUP WAS TOO LARGE. WE'LL SNEAK IN.
WELL, HERE WE ARE...

IT DOESN'T LOOK THAT BAD...
WHAT DID YE EXPECT? DARK LANDS? EXPLODING VOLCANOES? THAT'S ONLY IN THE STORIES YE HEAR...
WELL... LET'S BE ON OUR WAY.

IT'S BEST TO FLY AMONG THE CLOUDS AND FOG... THE BETTER FOR US TO GET PAST MUCH OF THE LAND BENEATH.
WHAT ARE ALL THOSE LIGHTS?
TORCHES... CAMPFIRES... THAT'S THE MONSTER ARMY BEING GATHERED BY OROGIGANTUM.
THERE'RE SO MANY...
IT WON'T BE LONG BEFORE THEY MARCH ON THE HUNDRED KINGDOMS.
THE ORACLE SAW THIS DANGER.
AHOO! WHAT DO WE HAVE HERE?

SNEAKING INTO THE CLOUD KINGDOM, ARE WE?
WHO ARE YE?
I AM THE LORD COMMANDER OF THE CLOUD CASTLE, LITTLE HAG.
WE ARE ON OUR OWN BUSINESS. LEAVE US BE.
OH, REALLY? I'M SURE OROGIGANTUM WILL BE PLEASED TO SEE YOU!
LORD COMMANDER! THAT'S NO ORDINARY HAG... SHE LOOKS LIKE...
AYE! MY EYES DON'T LIE! IT IS SHE!
IT'S MERCILESS MEM!
MERCILESS MEM?

MERCILESS MEM OF THE TERRIBLE EIGHT!
OH, YOU ARE A LEGEND, MADAM!
EEH!
YOU ARE AN INSPIRATION TO ALL WITCHES!
AYE... IT IS I.
MEM?
THAT'S RIGHT, MY DEAR... NOW, LET US BRING YOU TO OROGIGANTUM...
I THOUGHT YOU WERE OUR FRIEND!
!
NO USE RUNNING AWAY, PRINCESS. YOU ARE PRINCESS MABELROSE, AYE? BROOMS ARE FASTER THAN CARPETS. WE'LL ONLY CATCH UP WITH YOU...
IT WOULD BE OUR PLEASURE TO ESCORT YOU TO THE CLOUD CASTLE.
THAT WON'T BE NECESSARY, COMMANDER. HIS GREAT-NESS--
OH, BUT WE'RE HEADED THE SAME WAY.
LET'S BE ON OUR WAY, THEN.

HOW CAN YOU DO THIS, MEM? WE TRUSTED YOU.
QUIET. FACE FORWARD.
HEHEHEH. I BET YOU'LL TASTE GOOD IN MY STEWPOT, LITTLE CRITTER.
DON'T YOU DARE.
HEHEHEH! AND WHO'S GOING TO STOP ME? YOU? CHANCES ARE, OROGIGANTUM WILL TURN YOU INTO AN APPETIZER AS WELL, PRINCESS!
OROGIGANTUM DEMANDS, AND PEOPLE PAY.
SOMEONE WHO HAS COMMAND OVER LEGIONS OF FOLLOWERS DOESN'T NEED TO KIDNAP PRINCESSES FOR A FEW SACKS OF GOLD.
AH, HERE WE ARE...
BEHOLD...!

...THE IRON GATE. THE ENTRANCE TO THE CLOUD KINGDOM!
...

GUESTS FOR THE CLOUD CASTLE!
AYE, SIR LORD COMMANDER...
"THE IRON GATE IS OPEN FOR YOU."
HEHEHEH! WELCOME TO MY HUMBLE TOWER!

HAVE SOME WINE AND BREAD.
WE SHOULD BE GOING.
SOON ENOUGH, MADAM MEM. WE'LL BE MOVING OTHER PRISONERS ASIDE FOR OUR INTREPID PRINCESS MABELROSE.
I SENT WORD TO THE CASTLE FOR A HEAVIER GUARD. FOR NOW...
STAY A WHILE, PRINCESS!
HEY--!
I CAN DELIVER HER BY MYSELF.
OH, BUT I INSIST! SIT AND BE COMFORTABLE. THIS WON'T TAKE LONG.
WHAT DO YOU HAVE TO FEAR?
MUCH SAFER WITH GREATER NUMBERS, UNLESS... YES...
!

HEHEHEH... NOT SO FAST. I KNEW THERE WAS SOMETHING WRONG WHEN I SAW YOU FLYING ALONE.... THE GREAT MEM WOULD NOT BE FLYING WITHOUT A HORDE OF FOLLOWERS.
SO THE RUMORS ARE TRUE... YOU DID JOIN THE FAIRIES...
NONSENSE! OROGIGANTUM WILL HEAR ABOUT THIS! HE'LL--
YOU GAVE YOURSELF AWAY THERE, HEHEHEH...
I'M SURE OROGIGANTUM WILL BE AMUSED. A COMMON MISTAKE, UNLESS YOU'RE IN... HER... INNER CIRCLE? AHAHAHAH! IT IS HARD TO TELL, ADMITTEDLY, BUT YES...
...THE "LORD OF DRAGONS"... IS A QUEEN. NOW, TO THE DUNGEONS WITH Y--
EH?
AWK!
AWK!
AWK!

AAH!
WHUMP
OOF!
AWK!
AWK!
AWK!
TWING
AIEE!
OUH!
AAANH!
OUCH! HOW RUDE!
stomp

COME HERE!
AAA!
WHERE IS SHE?
OUR EYES!
I HAVE YOU NOW!
ZWING
AIEE!
TLORP
SLIPPERY FEET, BUTTERY SHOES!
AIEEE!
TILILING

KRAK
AAAAAAAAAAIEEEEEE
SPLASH
OOOH! I'M FALLING! OOF!
AGH!
LET'S GET OUT OF HERE!
I'LL GET THE BROOMS.
HEY, THAT ROPE'S MOVING! IT'S MOVING!
WHUMP
OWHP!
THAT'S OUR FRIEND.

NO, NO! BROOMS AREN'T LIKE CARPETS! THEY RECOGNIZE THEIR OWNERS!
OUCH! NOW YOU TELL ME.

PRINCE INGLE! YOU CAME BACK!

PRINCESS.
?

GAZE!
WAIT-- IRON TO WOOD!

THANKS.

INTO THE BRAMBLE FOREST. DON'T FLY.

UM... I BELIEVE THE HUNDRED KINGDOMS...
...ARE THAT WAY?
WE SHOULD BE SAFE FOR NOW.
YOU'RE PRINCESS MABELROSE.
YES. AND YOU?
I'M GAZE. AN HONOR TO MEET YOU, PRINCESS.
YE WERE SEPARATED FROM THEM?
ESCAPED BEFORE WE WERE BROUGHT UP TO THE CLOUD CASTLE. THE OTHERS WERE FLOWN UP THE NEXT DAY.
TOO MANY MONSTERS. NOTHING I COULD DO.
BIG DRAGON'S MINIONS DID NOT KNOW I CAN PICK LOCKS ON CHAINS.
HID FOR MANY DAYS. HOPED THE SEARCH WOULD BE CALLED OFF. LORD COMMANDER AND WITCHES CAUGHT ME.

YOU ESCAPED TOO, MEM?
YES... BUT I... I DID NOT KNOW WHETHER TO RETURN TO THE FAIRY LANDS OR...
COME AFTER THEM?
AYE... I JUST WANDERED AROUND FOR DAYS, UNABLE TO DECIDE WHAT TO DO NEXT...
DON'T BE TOO HARD ON YOURSELF, MEM. YOU WERE ALONE.
COME. CAN'T STAY IN ONE PLACE.
WAIT...
P-PRINCE GAZE, WE CAN'T GO HOME YET. I--
I KNOW. YOUR FATHER.
UM... YES.
WE'LL NOT LEAVE WITHOUT THEM.
ALL OF THEM. I PROMISE.
BRAMBLE FOREST WILL END SOON.

...CLOUD CASTLE IS STILL FAR AWAY TO THE SOUTH. TOO MUCH OPEN LAND.
SEE? NO PLACE TO HIDE.
WHAT IS IT, SPIKY?
SOMETHING'S COMING!

BMMM
RAWK
RAWK
BMMM
RAWK
RAWK
BMMM
BMMM
BMMM

EVERYONE...
"LET'S GET OUT OF HERE"?
WE HIDE AND WAIT.
OH, BOTHER. I KNEW YE'D SAY THAT.

THAT'LL BE OUR WAY IN.
WHAAAT? B-BUT THERE'RE GIANTS!
WHEN A BIG DUST CLOUD COMES, STAY LOW AND FOLLOW ME.
HURRY, HURRY NOW!

MABELROSE, WE CAN--
I GOT THIS. FOLLOW ME UP!
HNH!
OW, MY ARMS! IT'S BEEN A WHILE...

AS I WAS SAYING...
...I WAS GOING TO SAY WE CAN COME UP LIKE THIS.
?!
...
PRINCE INGLE, I... I'M SORRY--
NO, I SHOULD BE THE ONE TO ASK YOUR PARDON.

I SHOULD NOT HAVE LEFT YOU TO FACE DANGER ALONE. I'M SORRY.

THANK YOU FOR COMING BACK, INGLE. AND FOR RESCUING US... AGAIN.

HMM, THAT'S RIGHT! THAT'S TWICE NOW I'VE RESCUED YOU. MAYBE I'VE EARNED...

...MY REWARD?
SMOOCH
THANK YOU FOR RESCUING US!
...
HOW LONG DO WE HIDE HERE?
AS LONG AS IT TAKES.
CARAVAN SUPPLIES CASTLE.
IF WE'RE LUCKY, THIS CARAVAN WILL TAKE US TO THE CLOUD CASTLE, THEN?
"IF."
FEEE! FIIIEE!
FEEE! FIIIEE!
WHAT IS THAT?
THE "IF."

FEEE, FIIIEE, FO, FUM...
FEEE, FIIIEE, FO, FUM...
THE ONE-EYED... THEY HAVE THE EYES OF AN EAGLE.
WE'RE DOOMED.
THEY SEE EVERYTHING... STAY IN THE SHADOWS, EVERYONE.
UH-OH! HIDE, HIDE!
FEE, FIE... FEE, FIE...

UM... ONE JOLT AND I COULD FALL. ARE YOU SURE THERE'S NO ROOM THERE?
NO ROOM, SORRY. ASK THE GIANTS IF YOU CAN SLEEP ON THE WAGON BED.
WHAT ABOUT YOU, GAZE?
I'LL KEEP WATCH.
I'M GLAD YOU'RE ALL WITH ME. GOOD NIGHT, EVERYONE.
GOOD NIGHT.
SNARK...
GOOD NIGHT, SPIKY.
GOOD NIGHT.
GOOD NIGHT, PRINCESS.
FEEE, FIIIEE, FO, FUM...
FEEE, FIIIEE, FO, FUM...
WAKE UP, MABELROSE!
COME AND LOOK!

I-IT'S A BEANSTALK! A WHOLE FIELD OF THEM!
PATH TO THE CLOUD CASTLE...
"WELL TRAVELED, WELL GUARDED."

HALT!
?
STOP THE CARAVAN!
WE HAVE RUNAWAY PRISONERS ON THE LOOSE. SEARCH EVERY WAGON!
WE'RE LOOKING FOR A PORCUPINE, A SMALL WITCH, A GIRL, A BOY, AND A... KID WITH SNAKES FOR HAIR.
AYE, MILORD.
OH, NO... HE'S GOT SNIFFERS.
SNIFFERS? THAT DOESN'T SOUND GOOD.
CAPTAIN... SMELL THEM OUT!
SNIFF
SNIFF
SNIFF

SNIFFFF
FEE, FIE... FEE, FIE, FO, FUM...
FEE, FIE, FO, FUM! I SMELL THE BLOOD OF THE LITTLE 'UNS! BE THEY ALIVE OR BE THEY DEAD...
I'LL GRIND THEIR BONES TO MAKE ME BREAD!
WE HAVE THE SCENT! BRING THEM TO ME!

HURRY, PUT ON THE WINTER BLOOMS! THEY'LL COVER YER SCENT!
WHY DON'T YOU PUT FLOWERS ON?
WHAT DO I SMELL LIKE?
SNIF SNIF
SNAKES!
SCENT'S BECOMING WEAK, LORD COMMANDER.
WHAT DO YOU MEAN, THE SCENT IS WEAK? FIND THEM!
WELL, WHERE ARE THEY?

REPORT! HAVE YOU FOUND THEM YET?
WE LOST THE SCENT, SIRE.
WHAT HAPPENED?
UR... CAN'T SMELL ANYTHING EXCEPT WINTER BLOOMS.
WINTER BLOOMS?! YOU NINCOMPOOP! DO YOU SEE MOUNTAINS HERE? THEY'RE WEARING THE WINTER BLOOMS!
GO FOLLOW THE WINTER-BLOOM SMELL AND YOU WILL FIND THEM!
AYE, AYE, SIRE! RIGHT AWAY!
WELL, THEY DID MASK YOUR SCENT...

WHAT NOW? WE CANNOT OUTRUN GIANTS!
I'M THINKING.
WE'VE LEFT THE FLOWERS BEHIND... BUT THEY CAN SEE OUR TRACKS.
YOU DON'T LEAVE ANY FOOTPRINTS! HOW--?
HER BOOTS ARE FROM THE DRAGON'S TREASURE.
ALONE, I LEAVE NO TRAIL. MEM FLOATS AND LEAVES NONE... SPIKY'S FEET LOOK JUST LIKE ANY OTHER ANIMAL TRACKS...
I'LL LEAD THEM AWAY FROM YOU, PRINCESS.
HOW WILL WE--
I WILL FIND YOU.
I'LL COME WITH YOU. WE'LL LEAD THEM ON A MERRY CHASE.

WHAT ABOUT ME?
TURN INTO A FROG.
I CAN'T CONTROL MY CURSE!
MEM, SCARE HIM, QUICK.
RAARH!
W-WHAT ARE YOU DOING?
FEAR.
NGSSSSS
Aaaaah!
TOO MUCH?
WELL, IT WORKED.

BEHIND YOU ARE FOUR BEANSTALKS CLUSTERED AS ONE. WE'LL MEET UNDER ITS ROOTS.
GOOD LUCK AND STAY SAFE.
TRACKS OVER THERE!
THEY GO IN THE WATER.

STAY DOWN! WHAT ARE YOU DOING?
DOING WHAT I DO BEST.
FEE, FIE, FO--
OBEY.
FEE... FEE, FIE, FO... AYE... I OBEY...
WHAT YOU SEE?
ALL TRACKS GO NORTH. GET THE OTHERS.

UHH... WHAT HAPPENED? SNAKES...
SO THAT'S HOW HE TURNS BACK...
I SMELL WINTER BLOOMS THIS WAY!
THE BLOOMS' SCENT IS STILL IN OUR CLOTHES!
WE'LL HAVE TO COVER IT UP SOMEHOW!
HEY... YES... IT'S ALL OVER THE PLACE.
GIANT OX DROPPINGS MASK ANY SCENT.
HURRY! SMEAR SOME ON YOURSELF!
COME ON! THE STENCH WILL REMOVE THE FLOWER SMELL!
NO! GET THAT AWAY FROM ME!
THUMP
SPLAT
AHH!
BETTER A LITTLE DIRTY THAN CAUGHT.
A "LITTLE DIRTY"?!

FLOWER SCENT GONE, LORD COMMANDER.
UR... LOST SIGHT OF THE TRACKS TOO... THEY GONE.
YOU BUNCH OF BUFFOONS! CAN'T YOU DO ANYTHING RIGHT?
GET OUT OF HERE AND GET ME ANOTHER BATTALION!
GET ME MORE SPOTTERS AND SNIFFERS! FALL BACK AND REASSEMBLE! SEARCH THE SURROUNDING AREAS!
FIND THEM OR OROGIGANTUM WILL BURN YOU ALL!
MOVE OUT!
SEARCH HAS MOVED ON, PRINCESS MABELROSE.
GOOD TO SEE YOU BOTH.
...

THE CLOUD CASTLE IS UP THERE, SOMEWHERE.
THAT'S A LONG WAY UP.

LUCKILY, WE DON'T HAVE TO CLIMB!
W-WHAT? WHY DOESN'T THE CARPET WORK?
I WAS AFRAID THIS WOULD HAPPEN.
WHY WON'T THE CARPET FLY, MEM?
HUGE BEANSTALKS DRAIN A LOT OF MAGIC FROM AN AREA WHERE THEY ARE PLANTED.
WE WOULDN'T MAKE IT, IN ANY CASE. THAT ISN'T A CLOUD RIDER.
YOU CANNOT BE SERIOUS?! YOU MEAN WE'LL CLIMB THAT GIANT VINE TO THE CLOUDS?
LET US GO, THEN. WE HAVE A ROPE. WE CAN DO THIS.
THERE'S NO WAY... CLIMB UP THERE? ON FOOT? THAT'S IMPOSSIBLE. SHE'S JUST IMPOSSIBLE.
I LIKE HER.

THANK YOU FOR GUIDING US THIS FAR, MEM.
I CANNOT FLOAT AS OFTEN NOW. I HOPE I'M NOT SLOWING US DOWN.
YOU AREN'T.
SAVE YOUR FLIGHT FOR WHEN WE NEED YOU TO TIE THE ROPE.
AT LEAST WE'RE ALSO SAFE FROM THE WITCHES ON BROOMS.

!
HOW FAR UP DO WE STILL HAVE TO GO?
...WE'RE RUNNING OUT OF FOOD AND IT'S GETTING REALLY COLD.
WON'T BE FAR NOW, I THINK. I HAVE SOMETHING THAT SHOULD CHEER US UP.
OH! TRICIA'S PUMPKIN PIE!

WE'RE RUNNING OUT OF FOOD.
LEAVE THAT TO ME.
WHAT ARE YOU DOING?
LISTENING FOR OUR FOOD...
TAP TAP
YES, THIS SOUNDS ABOUT RIGHT.
HERE WE GO! A BANQUET OF DELIGHTS!
OOH! TASTY!
EUGH! I CAN'T EAT THAT!
IT'S WHAT I EAT WHEN I'M A FROG. THEY'RE GOOD.
YOU'RE A PRINCE AFTER MY OWN HEART, INGLE!
WISH THOSE STUCK-UP FAIRIES COULD SEE ME NOW...
TOMORROW WE'LL FIND YOU SOME MORE FOOD.
REAL FOOD THAT PEOPLE EAT.

ACHOO!
GESUNDHEIT.
LOOK!
WE'RE HERE! WE MADE IT!

OH, HELP...
WE ARE GOING INTO A DANGEROUS PLACE. I WON'T ASK YOU TO COME WITH ME.
WE'RE WITH YOU, PRINCESS.
I CAN'T VERY WELL CLIMB BACK DOWN, CAN I?
SPIKY, KEEP YOUR NOSE ALERT FOR ANY SCENTS.
I WILL.
MEM?
BEANSTALK DRAINED MY WAND. IT WILL RECOVER WHEN WE LEAVE THIS AREA.
STAY CLOSE TO US.
PRINCE INGLE, YOU--
I-I'LL BRING UP THE REAR! HEH!
WITH YOUR LEAVE, PRINCESS, I WILL LEAD US IN.
THANK YOU, GAZE.

STAY HERE. I'LL CLEAR OUR PATH.
ALL CLEAR, PRINCESS. COME TO THE GATE.
COME, RATLINGS WON'T WAKE UP.
ZZZZZ
HOW LONG WILL THEY SLEEP?
THREE DAYS IF THE SPELL ISN'T BROKEN.
ZZZZZ
IT'S EMPTY... W-WHERE ARE ALL THE GUARDS?
I DON'T THINK OROGIGANTUM NEEDS THAT MANY GUARDS, DEAR...
OH, HELP...

WHERE DO WE BEGIN?
THIS PLACE HAS VERY FEW SMELLS... MOSTLY OLD... MOSTLY RATLINGS... A FEW GIANTS... OH... THE SMELL OF FIRE...
SNIF SNIF
AAAAA...
SOUNDS LIKE SOMEONE'S IN TROUBLE.
OR IN PAIN.
I-I DON'T LIKE THIS...

NOOOO...
IT'S COMING FROM IN THERE...
WAIT HERE.
SLEEP.
OH, MERCY! MERCY! OOH...
ZZZ
ZZZZZ
ZZZ
COME.
OH, NO MORE... PLEASE...
...I BEG YOU!
SSSSSSSS

PLEASE. THERE'S ONLY SO MUCH I CAN STAND... PLEASE STOP!
WUHAHAHA!
SEARED AND CHARRED TO PERFECTION. AND IT'S ALL MINE!
YOU WANT A TASTE OF THIS? HEHEH!
YES... UHH... I'M SO HUNGRY! JUST ONE BITE.
BAH! GIANT BLACK OX FED ON BEANSTALK LEAVES IS TOO GOOD FOR YOU.
BEANSTALK FED? HOW CAN YOU BE SO CRUEL AND TEMPT US LIKE THIS?
SEASONED WITH GARLIC AND PEPPERCORNS TOO... CAN YOU SMELL IT? HEHEHEH!
ROASTED WITH GARLIC AND PEPPER-CORNS?! OOOH... YOU ARE DIABOLICAL!
AHIHIHEE! HEEEHEE!
LET THEIR MOUTHS WATER MORE, BOSS!
HEEEHEE
BEG ALL YOU LIKE!
YOU AIN'T--
gulp!
WHA--?

WHY, YOU--!
MUNCH
MUNCH
CHOMP
MUNCH
MUNC
CHIIING
!
WHACK!
!

EVERYONE...
...THIS IS EATER, SON OF CHIEF BIG-EATER.
AND THIS IS HIS COUNTERPART, BIG GULP.
THE PRINCESS! WOO! WOO!
EATER. PRINCESS MABELROSE.
OH, UH, GREETINGS...
THESE ARE PRINCE INGLE AND MY FRIEND SPIKY.
MEM IS WITH US, AS YOU CAN SEE.
THREE PRINCES! OOH, OUR CHANCES JUST GOT BETTER.

I THOUGHT SHE'D BE PRETTIER.
SHHH!
UH, THAT'S...
...JUST HIS OPINION. LET'S GO FIND YOUR FATHER.
SHALL WE?
YES...
"...THE REST OF THE CASTLE AWAITS!"

OH!!!
MM-MH! I DO APOLOGIZE FOR EATING IN FRONT OF YOU...
I HOPE YOU DON'T LIKE PORCUPINES.
OR FROGS!
PAPA! ARE YOU HERE?
PA?
PAPA! WHERE ARE YOU?
OVER HERE...
HELP!
CAREFUL.
HELLO? WHO'S THERE?

OH, WHO--? OH, MY! HOLD ON, WE WILL FREE YOU!
MY LADY! WHAT A SIGHT YOU ARE FOR WEARY EYES!
I MUST SAY, YOU ARE A HUGE IMPROVEMENT OVER SEEING THE DRAGON QUEEN AND HER NASTY CRONIES...
HOLD ON, KIND SIR!
SPIKY, THE KEYS!
THANK YOU! THAT FEELS GOOD!
THOSE CHAINS MUST HAVE BEEN A BURDEN.
IT WASN'T SO BAD, MY LADY. THEY KEPT ME IN SHAPE, AT LEAST.
THESE ARE MY FRIENDS MEM, SPIKY, EATER, BIG GULP, INGLE, AND GAZE.
YOU HAVE QUITE A GROUP WITH YOU!
ARE YOU FROM LEPTIA?
WHY YES! DID YOU JUST COME FROM THERE? DO YOU HAVE ANY NEWS?
YES. KING ARGAILE RULES.
BLESS MY SOUL! IS IT REALLY SO? KING ARGAILE IS BACK! WHOSE ARMY CAME TO FREE LEPTIA?
NO ARMY...
JUST... US.

YOU MUST BE A COURAGEOUS PRINCESS TO HAVE FACED IRGERAT'S MIGHT! IT IS AN HONOR TO MEET YOU. SIR ARTEMUS AT YOUR SERVICE.
I'M PRINCESS MABELROSE FROM THE KINGDOM OF NEW TINSLEY.
LO! THOSE STITCHES! I RECOGNIZE THAT STYLE!
M-MY WIFE IS THE BEST SEAMSTRESS IN ALL OF LEPTIA.
SHE IS THAT. AND A DEAR FRIEND.
YOU MET TRICIA! S-SHE IS SAFE, THEN? AND WALLY?
SHE AND YOUR NEPHEW WALLY ARE IN GOOD HANDS.
SHE WAS AMONG THE VERY FIRST WHO WELCOMED ME TO LEPTIA.
OH, SHE'S BEING MODEST. PRINCESS MABELROSE FREED ARGAILE AND YOUR PEOPLE FROM KING IRGERAT.
YOU FREED MY PEOPLE! OH, MY CUP IS FULL AND MY VERY HEART REJOICES! WITH THE KNOWLEDGE THAT MY DEAR WIFE AND HOMELAND ARE SAFE, ALLOW ME TO AID YOU IN YOUR QUEST!
I CAN SMELL GIANTS!
THEY'RE COMING.
FEE, FIIIEEE, FO, FUM...
IS EVERYONE READY?
WE'RE WITH YOU.

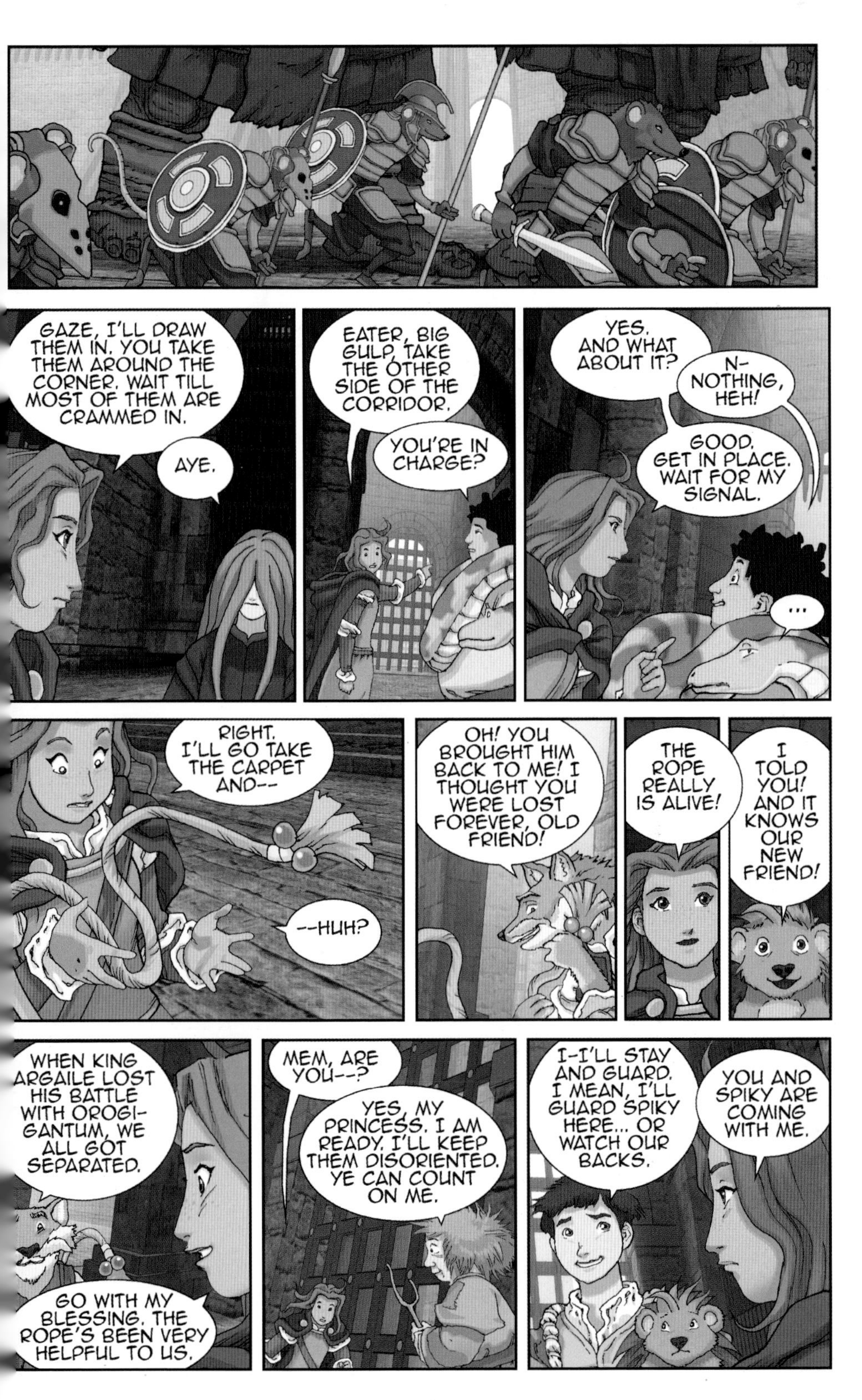
GAZE, I'LL DRAW THEM IN. YOU TAKE THEM AROUND THE CORNER. WAIT TILL MOST OF THEM ARE CRAMMED IN.
AYE.
EATER, BIG GULP, TAKE THE OTHER SIDE OF THE CORRIDOR.
YOU'RE IN CHARGE?
YES. AND WHAT ABOUT IT?
N-NOTHING, HEH!
GOOD. GET IN PLACE. WAIT FOR MY SIGNAL.
...
RIGHT. I'LL GO TAKE THE CARPET AND--
--HUH?
OH! YOU BROUGHT HIM BACK TO ME! I THOUGHT YOU WERE LOST FOREVER, OLD FRIEND!
THE ROPE REALLY IS ALIVE!
I TOLD YOU! AND IT KNOWS OUR NEW FRIEND!
WHEN KING ARGAILE LOST HIS BATTLE WITH OROGIGANTUM, WE ALL GOT SEPARATED.
GO WITH MY BLESSING. THE ROPE'S BEEN VERY HELPFUL TO US.
MEM, ARE YOU--?
YES, MY PRINCESS. I AM READY. I'LL KEEP THEM DISORIENTED. YE CAN COUNT ON ME.
I-I'LL STAY AND GUARD. I MEAN, I'LL GUARD SPIKY HERE... OR WATCH OUR BACKS.
YOU AND SPIKY ARE COMING WITH ME.

FEE, FIE, FO, FUM! I SEE A MAID AND HER LITTLE 'UNS!
WERE YOU EXPECTING SOMEONE ELSE?
I CALL UPON YOU TO SURRENDER!
WE HAVE PLENTY OF STRONG ALLIES. GIVE UP PEACEFULLY AND BE TREATED WELL.
AND IF WE REFUSE? WHAT WILL YOU DO THEN, LITTLE GIRL?
ASK MORE POLITELY?

AIEEE! WE'RE GONNA BE GIANT STEW NOW!
HOLD ON, PRINCE INGLE!
HURRY! FASTER!
GET THEM! GET THEM!
NOW!

AAOCH! THE GIANT SLAYER!
HE'S LOOSE! THE TAILOR IS LOOSE!
THIS IS FOR KEEPING ME HUNGRY ALL THAT TIME!

THAT'S IT, LAD! KEEP THEM OFF-BALANCE!
FEAR!
AAAIIEE!
GET THEM, INGLE!
Tonk!
!
DIZZY-TIZZY!

PHALANX FORMATION! RUN HIM DOWN!
?!
HOLD ON.
KRRRUMP!
MY THANKS, FROG PRINCE.
WISH I HAD NUTMEG FOR YOU!
LOOK OUT!
whump!

HRAAAHH...
AH... FRESH AND LIVELY MEAT!
IS THAT A PRINCESS WITH HER PRINCES I SMELL?
OUR BRAVE LITTLE TAILOR LOOSE? EVEN BETTER EATING...
IT'S OROGIGANTUM!
WE'RE DONE FOR!
SNAKES AND FAIRIES... ALL DELICIOUS...
WORRY NOT! WHATEVER COMES THROUGH THAT DOOR WILL BE EATEN WHOLE!
GIVE US A FEW MORE MOMENTS!

KOOMM
GET BEHIND ME, PRINCESS MABELROSE.
?
!
!

SSSSSS
GAZE!
STONE!
HRAAAHH...
NOOO!

YOU DID IT, GAZE!

GAZE DID IT... TURNED OROGIGANTUM TO STONE.

UH...

GAZE!

HE'S ASLEEP. HE'LL BE FINE.
THE EFFORT MUST HAVE COST HIM DEARLY. AT LEAST OROGIGANTUM IS OUT OF THE WAY NOW.
IT GRIEVES ME TO SAY THIS...

THAT DRAGON WAS VELDEROTH... OROGIGANTUM IS MUCH, MUCH LARGER...
WE MUST MOVE, THEN. IS EVERYONE READY?
YES, LET'S GO FIND YOUR FATHER.

FATHER!
PAPA?
WHERE ARE THEY? WE SEARCHED EVERYWHERE...

N-NOT EVERYWHERE, MABELROSE...
?
OH, HELP ME...

I SUPPOSE WE HAVE NO CHOICE THEN...
STAY LOW. OROGIGANTUM MAY BE WATCHING.
WE DO HAVE A CHOICE. RUN AS FAST AS WE CAN.
I'M NOT LEAVING WITHOUT M FATHER OR THE OTHERS.
YOU WANT TO GO AGAINST THAT?! WE'LL BE CAUGHT FOR SURE!

HOW ARE WE GOING TO EVEN APPROACH THAT?
LEAVE THAT TO ME.
I HAVE A PLAN...
LOOK! HERE COME MORE GIANTS!
FEE, FIIIEE, FO, FUM...
FEE, FIIIEE, FO, FUM...
FEE, FIIIEE, FO, FUM...
I CAME HERE NOT TO COME CLOSER TO THAT!
WE COULD GET CAPTURED!
IF WE FREE THE REST, WE HAVE A BETTER CHANCE OF ESCAPING... ALL OF US.
FIND A LARGE SHEET OF CLOTH AND GET SOME LONG POLES. WE DON'T HAVE MUCH TIME.

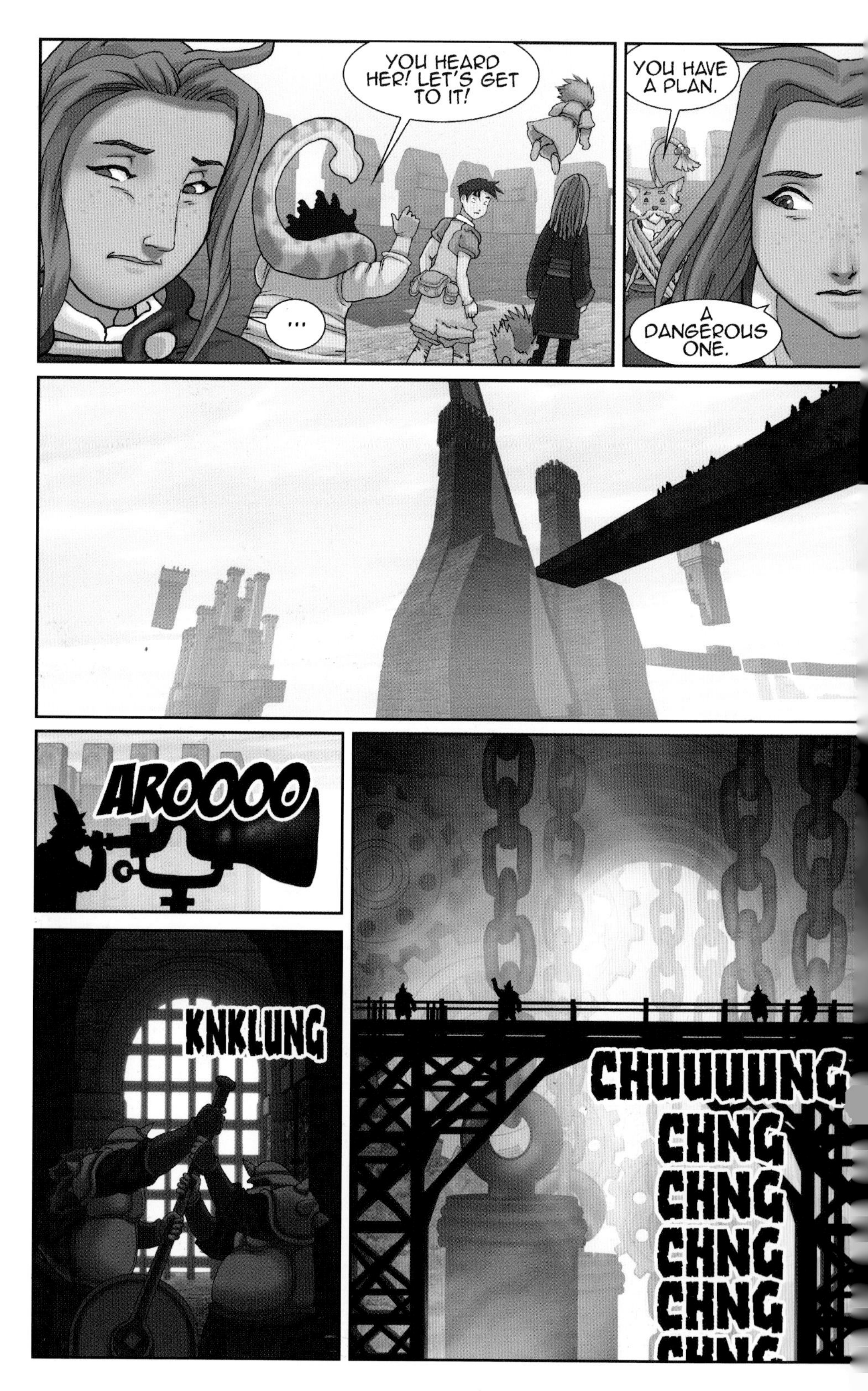
YOU HEARD HER! LET'S GET TO IT!
...
YOU HAVE A PLAN.
A DANGEROUS ONE.
AROOOO
KNKLUNG
CHUUUUNG
CHNG
CHNG
CHNG
CHNG

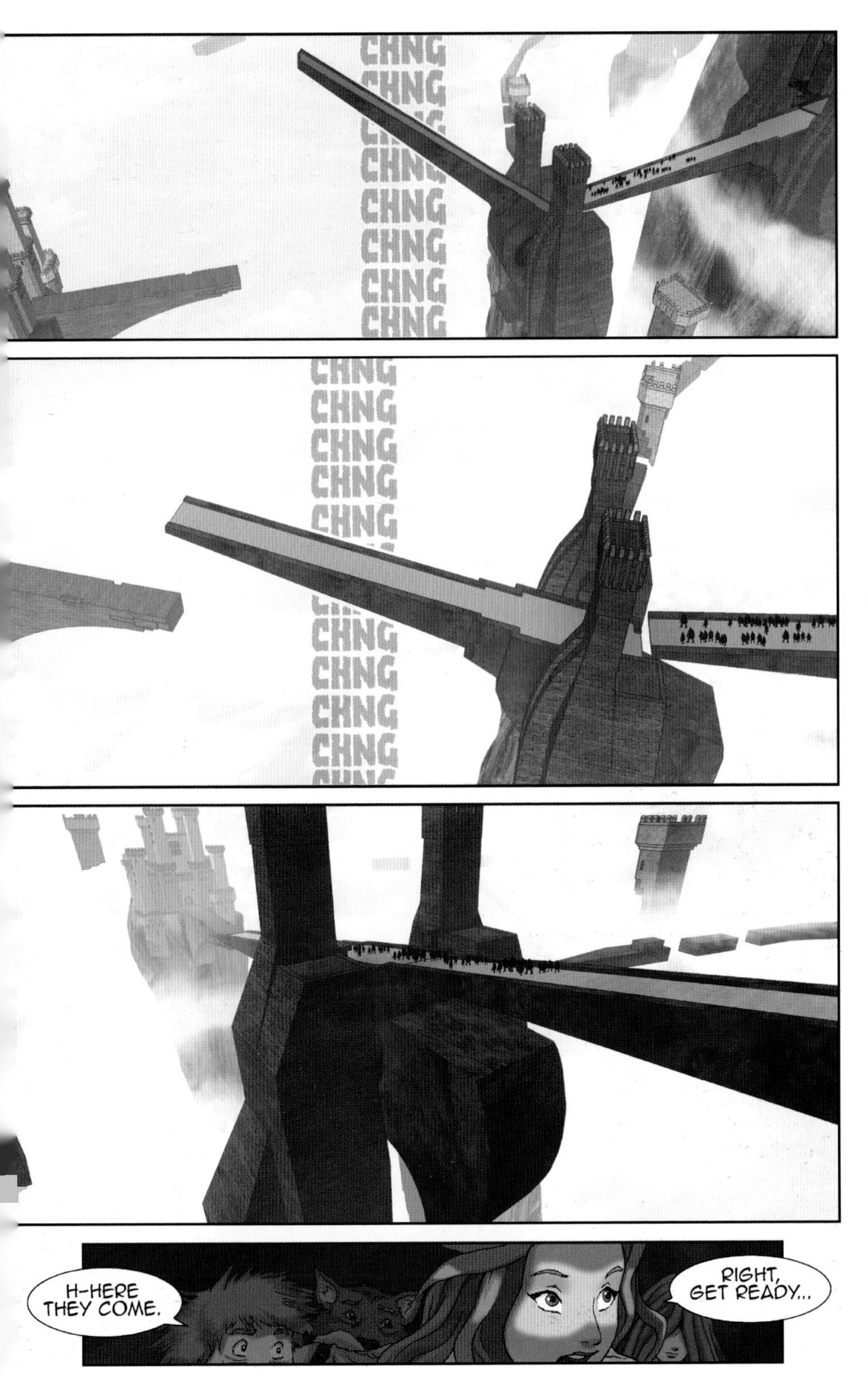
CHNG
CHNG
CHNG
CHNG
CHNG
CHNG
CHNG
CHNG
CHNG
CHNG
CHNG
CHNG
CHNG
CHNG
CHNG
CHNG
CHNG
H-HERE THEY COME.
RIGHT, GET READY...

THIS IS IT, EVERYONE.
READY.
READY TO MARCH.
READY, YOUR HIGH-NESS.
READY.
READY.
RIGHT, THEN... LET'S GO.
BIG STRIDES... BIG STEPS...

I HAVE A BAD FEELING ABOUT THIS!
STAY CALM. STEADY NOW.

AAAH! OH, NO!

WHERE ARE YOU GOING?

HNNGH!
SHHH...

...

WELL?

GRAAH! I GO TO REPORT TO THE CASTLE!
THEY FREED THE PRISONERS!
ERRK...
THEY'RE HOLDING THE UPPER TOWERS!
WE'LL SEND MORE REIN-FORCEMENTS.
YOU MAY GO TO THE CASTLE AND REPORT.
ALMOST THERE...
...

NO... NO...
HE CAN SEE US... WE'RE OUT IN THE OPEN...
H-HE CAN SEE US... OROGIGANTUM CAN SEE US!
SHHH!
plink
?!
THE HELMET! BIG GULP! THE HELMET!
...
!
!
!
HNNKH!
...

COME NOW, LITTLE ONES. NO NEED TO HIDE. I SEE YOU.
IT'S OROGIGANTUM!
CHUUUUING
COME... COME IN.
CHNG CHNG CHNG CHNG
AIEEEEEEEEEE!
CHNG CHNG CHNG
CHNG CHNG CHNG CHNG CHNG
AAAAAAAAAAAA!

BDUMMM
WELL, WELL, WELL...
WHO DO WE HAVE HERE? WELCOME TO MY CLOUD CASTLE.
WHERE ARE THE REST?

ALL CLEAR.

THEY CLOSED THE GATE.
I HOPE THE OTHERS MADE IT.

IT'S NOT TOO LATE, MABELROSE. WE CAN STILL--
EVERYONE DEPENDS ON US NOW, MEM...

WE'LL FIND ANOTHER WAY IN...
THIS DRAINAGE TUNNEL WILL DO.
HOW DO WE FIND THEM WHEN WE GET THERE?
IF YOU HAVE SOMETHING OF YOUR FATHER'S, I CAN TRACK THE SCENT.
QUIET NOW... THE DRAGON QUEEN MAY HEAR US EVEN DOWN HERE.
MABELROSE... THE QUEEN... SHE... I...
ARE YOU ALL RIGHT, MEM?
I... WE...
WE'LL BE FINE. JUST FOLLOW ME.

WHICH WAY?
I CAN SMELL THE DUNGEONS AND YOUR FATHER DOWN THIS WAY.
THAT'S JUST OLD RESIDUE.
IT'S FRESH.
I CAN SENSE YOUR FATHER UP HERE. QUICKLY NOW!
I...
WOULD I LEAD YE TO THE WRONG PLACE? TRUST ME...
RESCUE THE REST. THIS WILL LEAD YOU TO US.
GOOD LUCK, SIR ARTEMUS!
I WILL FIND YOU FAST.

WE'RE GETTING CLOSER. IT DRAWS ME THIS WAY!
STAY CLOSE AND READY.
AHH! IT IS PULLING ME NOW! WE ARE REALLY NEAR!
HURRY! THIS WAY!

MEM! YOU'RE GOING TOO FAST...

MEM, WAIT FOR US!
CLOSE... REALLY CLOSE... THIS WAY... HURRY...

MEM?
I... I AM SO SORRY...

?!

WELCOME, PRINCESS MABELROSE.
I AM PLEASED YOU CAN JOIN US.

COME FORWARD, LOVE... AREN'T YOU GLAD TO SEE YOUR DEAR AUNTIE?

FZAAA
ANH!

MABELROSE!

STOP!
AHAHAH. AND WHO DO WE HAVE HERE? THE ONE WHO GOT AWAY.

I DO NOT WISH TO HARM YOU, YOUR GRACE.
NOR I YOU.

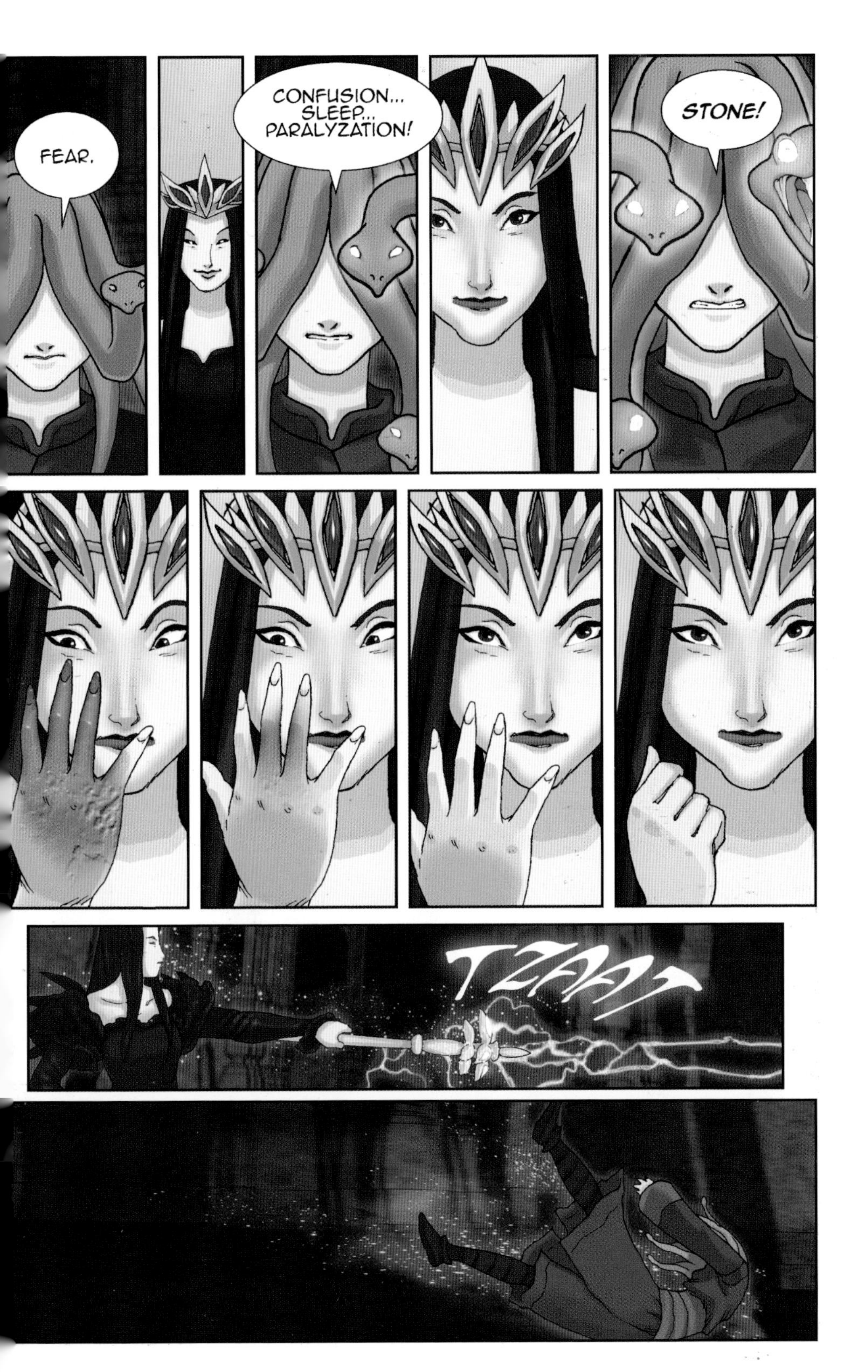
FEAR.
CONFUSION... SLEEP... PARALYZATION!
STONE!
TZAAT

AH, YES... YOU'VE GROWN UP, MY DEAR! IT'S BEEN YEARS!
A-AUNT URSULA? YOU... HOW...?
WELL, THEN... WHERE WERE WE?
BDAMM

P-PAPA!
THEY'RE WITH SIR ARTEMUS!
WE'RE SAVED!

MABELROSE! IT'S YOU! IT REALLY IS YOU!

PAPA! YES, IT'S ME!

THAT'S FAR ENOUGH.
URSULA! HOW COULD YOU? SHE'S ONLY A GIRL! LET HER GO!
EVENTUALLY. FOR NOW, RETURN TO YOUR QUARTERS AND NONE OF YOU WILL BE HARMED.
WE'LL PUT AN END TO YOUR SCHEMES FIRST!

TO BATTLE!
STOOOOP!

KING JERYK, GIVE UP THIS FIGHT OR YOUR DAUGHTER WILL SUFFER!

NO! YOU CAN'T! NOT EVEN YOU CAN BE THAT CRUEL! URSULA, FOR THE LOVE YOU BEAR YOUR FAMILY, DON'T DO THIS!

SURRENDER... OR ELSE...

GOOD.

OH, N-NO... N-NOT A-A-AGAIN...
YES, AGAIN, SHIVER. SHE HAS US.
...
...
LET THEM KEEP THEIR ARMS...
WHERE THEY'RE GOING, THEY WON'T BE OF ANY USE...
I'M SORRY, DEAR DAUGHTER.
F-FATHER...
BRING THEM TO THE PORTAL!

IT SEEMS NO CELLS IN MY CLOUD CASTLE CAN HOLD YOUR LITTLE BAND.
A MORE PERMANENT PRISON IS NEEDED.
THIS PORTAL IS A GATE TO THE LANDS OF NO RETURN.
I'M SURE YOU WILL HAVE A PLEASANT STAY.

PAPA... I... I'M SORRY... I FAILED.
YOU DIDN'T. I'M HAPPY TO SEE YOU AND THAT YOU ARE SAFE. I WILL FIND YOU AGAIN.
PRINCESS MABELROSE! I WILL COME BACK FOR YOU. YOU HAVE THE WORD OF PRINCE HEARFAR.
THANK YOU FOR COMING WITH MY FATHER, ALL OF YOU.
I WILL FIND YOU AGAIN. THIS, I PROMISE.
MY LADY, BE BRAVE. WE WILL ENDURE EVEN THIS. BE STRONG AND NEVER LOSE HOPE.
WE WILL COME BACK FOR YOU. YOU HAVE THE VOW OF PRINCE EATER, SON OF CHIEF BIGEATER.
YOU H-HAVE MY W-W-WORD AS W-WELL.
THANK YOU. ALL OF YOU.
W-WE SHALL RETURN! THIS I SWEAR W-W-WITH ALL M-MY H-HEART, W-WITH ALL MY SOUL, W-WITH ALL MY--

BAH, GET IN THERE!
PRINCESS MABELROOOOOSE!
PUT THE REST IN!
HEHEHEH!
HA!
MABELROSE... IF ONLY YOUR MOTHER COULD SEE YOU... THE LITTLE GIRL THAT WAS TAKEN FROM US HAS GROWN INTO A LOVELY YOUNG LADY.
I AM HAPPY I SAW YOU, IF ONLY FOR A SHORT TIME.
THIS WON'T BE FOREVER. WE WILL BE TOGETHER AGAIN. BE STRONG FOR A LITTLE WHILE LONGER.

YOU WON'T GET AWAY WITH THIS.
I WILL... AND I HAVE.
I'LL SEE YOU AGAIN SOON, WITCH QUEEN.
THE ANIMALS TOO.
NO!
MABELROSE!

YOU CAN'T! HE'S ONLY A SMALL PORCUPINE! PLEASE!
LEAVE HIM ALONE! CAN'T YOU SEE HE CAN'T EVEN HARM YOU?
MABELROSE... WHAT WILL HAPPEN TO US?
PLEASE TAKE CARE OF HIM, INGLE.
I WILL, PRINCESS MABELROSE.
SPIKY, I AM SO SORRY...
PUT THEM IN!

BE BRAVE FOR ME, SPIKY!
PRINCESS MABELROSE!
AAAAAH!
LORD COMMANDER!
PRINCESS MABELROSE!
NOOO!

AHUHUH... AHUHUHUH...

YOU DID NOT EVEN ALLOW ME TO TOUCH MY FATHER...
COME... I WILL TAKE YOU TO YOUR ROOMS.

SHOULD YOU NEED ANYTHING, THERE WILL BE SERVANTS THERE TO ATTEND TO YOU.
I WILL SUMMON YOU TOMORROW.

BOOTS!
HERE, OLD FRIEND!
IS EVERYONE HERE? STAY TOGETHER NOW!
EVERYONE IS PRESENT AND ACCOUNTED FOR!
W-WHERE ARE WE?
WE ARE IN A REALM CALLED THE LANDS OF NO RETURN. YOU CANNOT WALK, SWIM, OR EVEN FLY BACK TO THE HUNDRED KINGDOMS FROM HERE.
YOU ARE MABELROSE'S FRIENDS. YOU WILL BE OUR FRIENDS.
LOOK, OVER THERE!

EEEYYY! HELLOOOO!
WHAT, WHO--?
NO CAUSE FOR ALARM, MY FRIEND. HE APPEARS TO BE A PRISONER HERE. AND IT LOOKS LIKE--
"--HE'S BEEN HERE FOR A LONG TIME."
WELCOME, MY FRIENDS! OH, BOY, OH, LORDY! IT'S GOOD TO SEE OTHER PEOPLE AGAIN. IT'S BEEN AGES! WELCOME TO THE OASIS OF PLENTY!
COME, COME! I BREWED A FRESH BATCH OF COCOA THIS MORNING.
COCOA DRINK!
T-T-TREES!
SHELTER! WE'RE SAVED.
UM... WE'VE ONLY BEEN IN THE DESERT FOR ALL OF TWO MINUTES...

HUZZAH! OASIS OF PLENTY, HERE WE COME!
JERYK OF NEW TINSLEY, GREAT-GRANDSON OF THE LAMP KING.
MY NAME'S JACK. JACK THE CLIMBER.
PUSS IN BOOTS.
WELCOME TO THE OASIS...
"...MAKE YOURSELVES AT HOME."
LOOKING OUT OVER THE HORIZON, THIS SOON?
IT'S BEST TO REST FOR NOW, MY FRIEND. THE ENDLESS DESERT ISN'T GOING ANYWHERE.
I SEE WE HAVE NEW COMPANIONS. COME FORWARD, FRIENDS.
THESE ARE PRINCE INGLE AND SPIKY.
IT'S AN HONOR TO MEE BOTH OF YOU. COME, LET US REST.

SPIKY, IS IT?
YOU'RE MABELROSE'S FATHER! I'M HAPPY TO FINALLY MEET YOU!
THE HONOR IS ALL MINE. I HAVE SO MANY QUESTIONS.
YOU'VE BEEN WITH HER SINCE SHE BEGAN HER JOURNEYS?
YES, WE HAVE.
ME AND OUR ROPE FRIEND THERE!
HE'S BEEN VERY HELPFUL.
BUT NOW... SHE'S ALL ALONE WITH THAT MEAN WITCH.
WE'LL SAVE HER SOMEHOW. I PROMISE.
TELL ME EVERYTHING YOU REMEMBER.
IT'S A LONG STORY.
WE'RE NOT GOING ANYWHERE. LOOKS LIKE WE HAVE ALL THE TIME IN THE WORLD.
WELL...

...I MET MABELROSE AT THE BRIAR FOREST, AT THE EDGE OF SHALATHRUMNOSTRIUM'S LANDS...
To be concluded...

COMING FROM DARK HORSE BOOKS

THE COURAGEOUS PRINCESS™

VOLUME 3

THE DRAGON QUEEN

The following pages are a special preview of the next volume of The Courageous Princess, *in which Mabelrose must again come to the rescue . . .*

.....!
LOOKING FOR SOMETHING?
OH!

WELL HELLO, MY DEAR.
W-WHERE DID YOU COME FROM?
THE QUESTION IS... WHERE ARE YOU GOING?
ARE YOU TRYING TO EQUIP YOURSELF FOR AN ESCAPE?
LET ME SHOW YOU WHY THAT'S A FOOLISH IDEA.
AAAH!
?!
!

FROM THIS CASTLE, THERE IS NO ESCAPE.
AAAH!
OUH!
AHA-HA-HA-HA HA-HA!
!

THAT WAS NOT FUNNY! WHAT IF IT ATE ME?
CALM DOWN. THE DRAGON IS UNDER MY COMPLETE CONTROL.
OH. HOLD ON TIGHT.
WHOAA!

!
ONE OF THESE CAN FEED A SMALL TOWN FOR A YEAR.

AND YOU HAVE A MILLION OF THEM --A BILLION!
AH-HN-HN! THIS HOARD IS NOT FOR THE FEEDING OF STREET URCHINS, PRINCESS.
YOU HAVE SO MUCH... WHY DO YOU WANT MORE?

THERE IS NEVER ENOUGH.
OH!
AAH!
AAAH!

Princess Mabelrose's adventures continue in The Courageous Princess *Volume 3:* The Dragon Queen*!*

Born in the Philippines and now residing in Texas, Rod Espinosa is the author and/or illustrator of more than forty-five comics and graphic novels for children and young adults. His wide range of work has covered everything from biographies of American historical figures, to graphic-novel adaptations of the works of William Shakespeare, Charles Dickens, and Lewis Carroll; from benefit books for the World Health Organization and the relief efforts for Typhoon Haiyan, to science fiction and fairy tales.

Rod's works have won him a number of nominations and awards from around the world:

2000—Ignatz Awards for Promising New Talent and Outstanding Artist for *The Courageous Princess*

2002—Eisner Award nomination for Best Title for Younger Readers for *The Courageous Princess*

2006—Max and Moritz Prize nomination for Best Comic for Children for *Neotopia*

2008—Winner of an international competition to be the artist for *Luís Figo and the World Tuberculosis Cup*, an educational comic book sponsored by the Stop TB Partnership and the World Health Organization

Along with all of his other projects, Rod is putting the finishing touches on the long-awaited third volume of his *Courageous Princess* trilogy.

OTHER BOOKS BY

ROD ESPINOSA

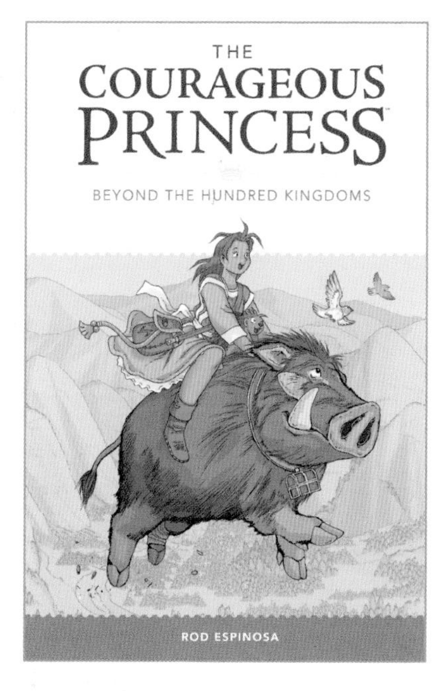

THE COURAGEOUS PRINCESS
VOLUME 1: BEYOND THE HUNDRED KINGDOMS
THIRD EDITION

Once upon a time, a greedy dragon kidnapped a beloved princess . . . but if you think she just waited around for some charming price to rescue her, then you're in for a surprise! Princess Mabelrose may not be the fairest of the land, but she has enough brains and bravery to fend for herself in a fantasy world of danger and adventure!

ISBN 978-1-61655-722-5 / $19.99

COMING SOON: **THE COURAGEOUS PRINCESS VOLUME 3: THE DRAGON QUEEN!**

ALICE IN WONDERLAND

The curious Alice follows a flustered white rabbit to a magical land of talking animals, evil queens, and enough riddles to strain any logically inclined brain.

ISBN 978-1-61655-046-2 / $19.99

A CHRISTMAS CAROL: THE NIGHT THAT CHANGED THE LIFE OF ELIZA SCROOGE

The miserly Eliza Scrooge is visited by the ghosts of the past, present, and future on one fateful Christmas Eve.

ISBN 978-1-59582-991-7 / $19.99